The Lion Mountains

M. L. Eaton

The beauty and spirit of Sierra Leone captivate a young English girl

To Adnan

with many thanks for all your help and support. I hope you enjoy this.

All good wishes

(M. L. EATON)

15 · 11 · 15

Copyright © 2015 M. L. Eaton

The right of M. L. Eaton to be identified as the author of this work has been asserted by her in accordance with the Copyright, Designs and Patents Act 1988. May all who read this book be richly blessed.

Published by Touchworks Ltd.
a company registered in England, no. 03668464.
Registered Office: 67 London Road, St. Leonards-on-Sea,
East Sussex TN37 6AR.

All rights reserved.
No part of this publication may be reproduced, stored in a retrieval system, or transmitted, in any form or by any means, electronic, mechanical, photocopying, recording or otherwise, without the prior permission of the copyright owner.

Also by M L Eaton

Mysterious Marsh series
#1 When the Clocks Stopped
#2 When the Tide Turned

Faraway Lands Series
#1 The Elephants' Child

Short Read
Norfolk Twilight

All books available in print and as e-books from Amazon including amazon.co.uk, amazon.com, amazon.com.au and amazon.in

A catalogue record for this title is available from the British Library.

- For -

My cousins Ursula and Christine

With fond memories of our shared childhood

'Semper aliquid novi Africam adferre'

'Africa always brings us something new'

Historia Naturalis
Pliny the Elder, AD 23 - 29
Roman Scholar

'What you help a child to love can be more important than what you help him to learn.'
African proverb

Prologue

The ripping, tearing sound grew louder. Another sound, like the padding of soft feet and the rasping of breath purposefully breathed. With a slight tug of resistance, the last of the tutu's stitches parted and she saw the tulle float past. The whirling stopped and she collapsed to the stage floor, panting. A sea of faces was staring down at her, so close that their breath was hot on her face. Hot, with the stench of rotten meat.

Where was she? A heartbeat later, she recognised the familiar soft mattress beneath her. Now she perceived the comforting walls of her bedroom around her. But she felt herself panting and her heart was beating unusually fast, her prone body instinctively reacting to impending danger. Something alive, something dangerous, something that even now was looming over her. Feeling the weight of it all around her, she dared not move, hardly dared to breathe. Holding her breath, she raised her eyelids enough to peer through her lashes — and quickly closed them.

Was she still dreaming? She knew she wasn't.

- 2 -
ATLANTIC OCEAN: JULY 1956

Melanie sniffed again.

For a moment she'd thought ... but it was the same old sea-smell. For the last few days, the viscous smell of the ocean had filled her lungs and clung to her skin.

She liked the smell, particularly the tang of ozone that made you feel happy and a little bit sleepy, but the stickiness of salt was another matter: she disliked it intensely and it was everywhere — on the ship's rail, on the outer sides of the deck doors and on the metal walls behind her mother's deckchair. If she tried, Melanie could walk all the way round the deck without touching anything at all, even when the ship was rolling and the waves were splashing over the bow. The sailors flung pails of fresh sea-water over the decks every morning: her mother explained they were 'swabbing the decks' which was another way of saying they were washing them down. But Melanie curled her lip and wrinkled her nose: the ship didn't smell clean. On the contrary, the entire exterior, especially the metal bits, reeked of salt and paint and an odd acrid smell that her mother said was diesel oil.

For two days now, the sea had been flat and blue and the sky had been flat and blue, too. When they had left the Canary Islands, the boat had danced a jig across the water and the plume of smoke that flew from its funnel had plunged and waved, torn by the wind. Today the ship's motion was smooth and monotonous: only the onward thrust of the motors kept the vessel moving through the limitless ocean. Melanie felt that she had been at sea forever. Perhaps that was what forever felt like — moving ever onwards across an empty, flat blue sea under an empty, flat blue sky....

A slight onboard breeze ruffled her curls — and suddenly she was encircled by an exotic fragrance. She closed her eyes and took a long, deep searching sniff. The fragrance teased her, tinging the air with an odour that was unnameable but tantalising, like the mixed aromas of flowers and petrol, or chocolate and firelighters. She climbed on to the ship's rail, all awareness of its stickiness sublimated to the intensity of the perfume that flirted with her senses, seducing her eight-year-old's consciousness with its muskiness.

"Careful, darling!"

Melanie felt her mother's breath brush her cheek.

"Can you smell it, Mummy?"

"What is it? Ah, it's Africa! I know the scent is intoxicating but we don't want you falling into the sea like a drunken sailor!"

Elizabeth Russell's hands gripped the ship's rail either side of her daughter.

"There. I've got you. You can climb up one more rung, but no more."

Startled, Melanie suddenly realised that she had unknowingly climbed up one forbidden level of the rail. Normally, she would just rest her chin on it leaving both feet firmly secure on the deck. Now her head was just above the parapet and Mummy had said she could climb even higher — and she wasn't cross. How exciting! Feeling the thrill of doing something previously forbidden, Melanie climbed up one more level.

"Lean into me, darling. Close your eyes. Now tell me what you can smell."

Melanie obediently leaned back into her mother's embrace, again closing her eyes the better to smell the fragrance.

"Rain ... wet earth ... no, trees after rain ... petrol, I think ... curry ... coconuts ... the sea ... hot skin ... flowers ... something like roses and jasmine, but even stronger."

Elizabeth chuckled. "Well described. I couldn't have done better myself. Anything else?"

"Muddy pond water."

Her mother let out a peal of laughter. "Absolutely right! And do you like the smell of Africa?"

"I'm not sure, Mummy," Melanie frowned. "I thought I liked it but ..."

A long way away something flashed: then came a long rumble. Like her tummy sometimes made, she thought, but louder.

"Was that lightning?" Elizabeth asked, before answering her own question. "It must have been! I heard thunder."

"There's something darker over there, Mummy like a navy blue cloud swimming in the sea."

"Where?" Elizabeth squinted in the direction indicated by Melanie's pointing finger. "I can't see

The Lion Mountains

anything, darling."

The air changed suddenly. It thickened, became more dense to breathe, and the floral smell increased, charged with pungent ozone. Driven by the squall, an ominous dark cloud raced across the sky, dimming the sun. The ship juddered as the storm hurtled towards the ship, huge raindrops striking small fountains from the heaving surface of the sea.

Elizabeth took Melanie's hand.

"Inside, darling. Quickly!"

Ten minutes later the squall had passed and soon afterwards most of the ship's passengers were back on deck.

"There's land off the port bow," the colonel reported to his wife, his clipped English accent perfectly pitched to carry.

Mrs Carey jumped. She was sitting in the deckchair next to Elizabeth and both women had been lost in their reading matter. Elizabeth was making no secret of the fact that she was absorbed in the plot of Agatha Christie's *The Murder of Roger Ackroyd*, while Mrs Carey appeared to be studying a large leather-bound volume entitled *Africa for Europeans*. A closer inspection would have revealed that within its pages she had concealed a thin paperback covered in brown paper. Its title thus hidden, only Melanie's eyes were young enough to read the small print at the top of each page: 'Fanny Hill'. Melanie thought that Fanny was a singular name for a hill – hills usually had interesting names like 'Malabar Hill' in Bombay. Or 'Bluebell Hill' or 'Chequertree Hill', both near her home in Kent, or steep 'Ide Hill', which Trevor, her brother, always swore was haunted by a carriage and four horses. Fanny was a girl's name, Melanie thought scornfully, and not at all interesting.

The colonel's call had roused his fellow passengers to action and by the time Melanie and her mother arrived they were thronging against the ship's rail. The Colonel beckoned them to his side. Melanie squeezed into the space he had saved for her in front of him. A thick blue-green splotch on the horizon showed where the African coast lay.

A shrill whistle sounded and a tinny voice could be heard through the speaking tube to the ship's bridge above them, where two of the ship's officers, their spotless tropical white uniforms ablaze with gold braid, stood rigid, legs braced apart against the motion of the ship.

"Aye, aye, sir."

The words rang down from the bridge and immediately the ship listed as it changed direction, causing no little consternation amongst the passengers clustered at the rail as they fought for a footing on the deck. Now the blue-green smudge was directly ahead. A seabird cawed overhead and Melanie looked up to see white-feathered birds lazily circling above the ship's churning wake. The wind was blowing shoreward, tearing at the slow oily waves and driving them onwards towards the shore.

"No wonder this used to be called 'The Windward Shore'," Elizabeth remarked, struggling to keep her full skirt under control as the wind whipped round the forecastle.

The Lion Mountains

"How right you are," Mrs Carey responded. She bent down to Melanie. "Listen Melanie — can you hear the surf pounding on the beach?"

Melanie held her breath and listened intently: sure enough, above the pulse of the engines and the rushing sound of the bow wave, she thought she could hear a deep rumbling thundery sound, like drums and cymbals together. She said as much to Mrs Carey who smiled and ruffled the little girl's blondish curls.

"What an observant daughter you have, Elizabeth!" Then turning to Melanie, she bent over a little and asked: "What do you know about Sierra Leone, my dear?"

"I know what Sierra Leone *means*," she informed the older woman. "Daddy told me. It's Portuguese for 'Lion Mountains'."

"And did your daddy tell you why the Portuguese gave it that name?"

"Yes! Because it thunders every day in the rainy season and the Portuguese thought lions were roaring in the jungle. He said the local people exaggerated this story to frighten the Portuguese away from the mountains. But when I asked the Captain, he said it was because Sierra Leone is shaped like a lion's head. He showed me the map — but I thought it looked much more like a cloud or a sheep than a lion."

Mrs. Carey suppressed a smile. "I agree with you. I like the roaring story much better. But look! We're coming closer to land."

Ahead of them, the blue-grey smudge was slowly changing into a definite shoreline above which jungle-clad slopes soared towards the sky. Melanie screwed up her eyes to see better: the foam of ocean breakers was just discernible against the yellow-white sand. The shore was empty of buildings, or indeed any sign of civilisation, but in the strengthening wind, Melanie could just make out a thick crust of dark green branches waving wildly, bending away from the sea. And now she could hear the pounding sea-sound of ocean rollers breaking on the beach. But the peculiar African smell was absent.

Again the bell on the bridge rang. One of the officers there stumbled a little as the helmsman brought the ship hard round to starboard. Once again the ship was running parallel to the shore, closer now, but heeling over to leeward.

Sheltering behind her mother from the sea wind, Melanie became aware of a sudden rustle of conversation and the words: "Freetown," "Over there," "On the horizon." Above her head, she felt an arm raised, its fingers pointing bow-wards, and she saw her mother squinting in the same direction. The passengers began to disperse. A happy smile lit up Elizabeth's face as she squatted down beside her daughter.

"We're nearly there, darling! In a few hours we'll be in Freetown! And Daddy will be waiting for us when we dock. Why are your eyes shut?"

The sun on the water made it difficult to keep your eyes open, Melanie said, and anyway she was trying to remember what Daddy looked like.

Behind her closed eyes, a picture of her father began to emerge. She saw his well-rounded figure clad in long shorts, long socks, and a white shirt open at the neck, its sleeves rolled up to his elbows. Her father's face, neck

The Lion Mountains

and forearms were burned almost black because he had spent so much time under the fierce sun of the tropics, but Melanie knew that when he took off his shirt, his upper arms and chest were pinkish-yellowish-white. She imagined him opening his arms and bending down to lift her high above his head so she could see the tanned bald patch surrounded by short greying hair. She remembered his infectious smile below the clipped moustache, his teeth shining whitely out of his tanned face; his wide nostrils narrowing as he took a drag at his cigarette; the sun glinting off the spectacles that masked his huge hazel eyes — eyes that were mostly amused but sometimes sad or thoughtful.

Melanie opened her eyes and tugged her mother's hand.

"Let's go to the bow, Mummy! I want to see. When will we be there? I can't wait to see Daddy!"

But the flat blue sea had once again become a rolling ocean. The risen wind, blowing landwards from the South — the direction in which they were travelling — created great troughs through which the ship pitched and wallowed, its ungainly progress and corkscrew motion causing several of the passengers to hurry below.

Neither Elizabeth nor her daughter suffered from seasickness. Together they stood at the prow of the ship, the wind tangling their hair as they gazed outwards.

Seabirds soared, shrieked and fought each other, before diving down into the ship's churning wake, the sun's rays catching the silver flash of a fish seized by a vicious beak. Melanie watched until her eyes ached. The sun danced mirror-like over the roiling indigo waves, its reflection breaking into a million glittering shards as the rollers dashed against the bow. The steady thrumming of the engines lulled mother and daughter into a reverie as the coast drew ever closer. Into the sky rose hills densely covered with jungle green of varying shades, light, bright and dark. Here and there a pop of scarlet, yellow or vermillion punctuated the dense vegetation as if surprised by its own brilliance. And occasionally, a window in the wind would free the evocative fragrance of Africa.

- 3 -

FREETOWN, SIERRA LEONE

Melanie's eyes were focussed on the wide bay that formed a natural harbour. Around the shore spread the port of Freetown on its peninsula, and now she could see the mouth of the great Sierra Leone river emptying its water into the ocean. Gradually the buildings grew in stature and more of the port spread out before their eyes. Along the wharfs that cut into the sea like great discoloured teeth, ant-like black people scurried back and forth. The ship steered towards the southernmost wharf where dockers were clustering close to a huge pile of tea-chests and lumpily-filled sacks.

White froth billowed and bloomed as the engines churned up the water, until, after much manoeuvring, the ship finally came to rest, her side gently scraping against the wharf. Black figures sped along the quay and shouts rang out as ropes were thrown, caught and secured to the bollards. Almost immediately, the passenger gangplank plunged down to the concrete dock. The towering necks of mechanical cranes extended as if alive and lowered their hooks into the cargo holds, which had miraculously opened. Like flowers on a sunny day after rain, Melanie thought.

And there, at last, was her father. Exactly as she had imagined him, with the sun glinting off his glasses. He had seen her! He was waving a huge bouquet of brilliantly hued flowers high above his head and his smile was broader than his moustache. She tumbled down the gangplank and threw herself into his arms. He lifted her high and swung her round, the flowers dropped unheedingly on the concrete quay. And then her feet were back on the ground and her arms were tight around his waist and he was embracing her mother and her as though he would never let them go, ever again.

As she slipped out from her parents' embrace, Melanie felt the atmosphere of the African port all around her. Amongst the usual smells of tar, oil and salt, the strange — and yet now somehow familiar — fragrance permeated the humidity. It was hot — much hotter than it had been on the ship. Hot moist air pressed down upon her and the blinding glare of the sun made her screw up her eyes.

Releasing her mother from his embrace, her father stooped to recover the bouquet of flowers, slightly crushed and already beginning to wilt in the heat. From beneath them, he produced a small parcel which he presented to his daughter with a flourish.

"You'll like this, sweetheart. Welcome to Africa!"

Tearing off the wrapping paper, she found a small furry lion.

"See here."

Her father took the toy from her and showed her how to turn the key in the lion's side. When he released it, the lion's mouth opened to reveal a red tongue and a strange humming sound came from inside. Melanie could feel the vibration.

The Lion Mountains

"It's a baby lion trying to roar," she cried, and jumped up and down in delight. "Thank you, Daddy!"

"It's a bit like Sierra Leone itself," her father remarked, *sotho voce,* to his wife. "Trying to roar before it's even left its mother."

Soon they were in the company car and a uniformed driver was steering them carefully out of the port and along the road into the centre of Freetown. Her parents were busy talking to each other and Melanie, gazing fascinated at all the new sights and sounds, allowed the dusty draught from the open window to lift her curls away from her sweaty brow.

The harbour and beaches surrounding the country's chief town were beautiful and almost deserted. Pale golden sands, fringed with coconut palms, stretched to rocky headlands from which the jungle tangled heavenward in a riot of green, while the sun glinted on calm azure waves from a sky of pellucid blue.

A bank of thick cloud swept down the mountains towards the sea enveloping in twilight the previously sunlit slopes. Melanie's hair bristled with static as a simultaneous crash of thunder and flash of brilliant white lightning rent the air. Then the rain fell. Even in the Indian monsoon, the little girl had never experienced anything like it. The car slowed. Melanie noticed the driver peering out through what seemed to be a waterfall, the windscreen wipers useless in the torrent.

"Pull over, Maurice," her father directed. "We have a precious cargo on board. We can wait until the rain lessens." As the car stopped, he turned to his daughter. "What a pity, sweetheart — I wanted to show you the

Cotton Tree, but we can't see anything in this downpour."

Melanie asked whether the Cotton Tree was really made of cotton and her father chuckled and shook his head.

"No, it's just its name. Cotton comes from a bush not a tree. You know that. We saw some in Pakistan. Do you remember?" Melanie nodded and her father continued. "The Cotton Tree is an important part of Freetown's history — and since Freetown is the capital of Sierra Leone, it's an important part of the whole country's history." He sighed and remarked to his wife. "It's amazing what a mess politicians can make, especially when they try to do good."

"What do you mean, Daddy?"

Harold stared ahead through the windscreen. The rain was still gushing down. There was nothing to be seen and driving along a perilous road up into the coolness of the mountains was unthinkable until the deluge was over. Now, he thought, was as good a time as any to introduce his daughter to a little of the region's history.

"A long time ago, when people were particularly cruel and unfeeling to others, there was a trade in people. It was called the slave trade …"

"I know all about slaves," his daughter interrupted. "I've been learning about the Romans and they captured prisoners wherever they went and turned them into slaves."

"So they did, Melanie. The principle was the same but this was trade, not war, and the slaves were treated abominably. They were packed into ships, shackled in lines beneath the decks so that they could barely move, fed on dreadful rations — if at all — and many fell sick and died. They died of disease, or cold, or grief, or all three. And when they died, or even if they were just very sick, they were thrown overboard to drown."

Elizabeth shuddered. "I'm not sure she needs to know all this yet, Harold."

Harold looked at his wife and something unsaid passed between them. Melanie's next words dropped into the silence.

"What's trade, Daddy?"

"Trade is when you exchange one thing for another. So you get something that you can sell for more money."

He paused and his mouth turned down at the corners. "It's always about money," he muttered.

"But how can you make money out of people? Especially if they are sick — or dead?"

Part of Harold wanted to applaud his little daughter's acumen, another part of him wanted to weep. He cleared his throat before he answered, noticing that his wife was regarding him warningly.

"I'll tell you more about the slave trade later, darling. Let's just say now that the slaves were sold and sent to work in plantations in America."

"But I want to know who was doing the trade," Melanie insisted.

Her mother shook her head.

"It's best to tell her the truth from the start, Elizabeth."

Elizabeth looked perturbed but said nothing. Perhaps

it was best to tell her now — just in case she met with animosity here in this unknown quantity of a country.

"The European nations, particularly Spain, France, Portugal and England …"

"England?" Melanie gasped. "But you've always told me England is 'the land of the free'!"

"Yes, England, too, I'm sorry to say. But keep listening because I haven't finished. To begin with, they took slaves from the people living in fishing villages on the coast. In fact, this has happened everywhere, throughout the ages. Fishing has been a dangerous occupation in more ways than one, even in England. The Barbary pirates of North Africa used to sail in and take away whole English communities that lived along the south coast. That was called the 'white slave trade'."

"Harold!"

Melanie's eyes were wide with horror. "But we live close to the sea! Will they …"

"No, darling. Daddy is talking of a long time ago. None of this happens now."

"I didn't mean to frighten you, sweetheart. As Mummy says, it was a long time ago, and we will never go back to those times and that dreadful trade. The English did the right thing in the end. They abolished slavery in all the British colonies and they forbade anyone with a trading base in Britain from engaging in the slave trade."

"That was *good*, wasn't it?"

"Yes, darling, it was. But they did even more than that. They tried to enforce their laws on all the other slave-trade nations. Can you guess where the British made their base?"

Melanie stuck out her bottom lip as she considered. "Here?"

"Precisely! Freetown was founded as a place where freed slaves could come back to their roots in Africa."

He pondered briefly. Should he also mention that there had been the freed slaves, known as the 'black poor' of London — nearly four hundred souls in total — who had founded a town here much earlier, in 1787 to be exact, but had perished within two years of their arrival in the colony? And that, though they were generations removed from their forebears who had originated in Africa, the British Government had sent them to start a new colony here in Sierra Leone? People who knew nothing of Africa, who were suffering from cold, who had travelled hundreds of miles in the vicious discomfort of a sailing vessel? What crass stupidity! No wonder that half of those first settlers had died in the first year, from tropical diseases from which they had no immunity. Several had found it sensible to throw in their lot with the native slavers. The survivors had been killed in 1789 by the indigenous inhabitants.

Harold heard himself sigh. It had been a well-meaning exercise, even though it had been fatally flawed; an experiment that paved the way for a much bigger exercise a few years later. And both of those attempts to use the place as a refuge for freed slaves had taken place before an Act of Parliament was passed in 1807 formally abolishing slavery in England. He decided that he would tell his daughter about that another time.

The rain began to ease: in less than a minute it had

ceased entirely. Immediately, the sun was shining down strongly, hotter by far than before. Ah! Africa! Its sunshine and promise disguised the primeval dangers beneath its surface, but there was no denying its latent power and potent allure. Africa's undeniable magnetism drew people of all kinds from all continents, remoulding them in some indefinable manner, as its raw power entered deep into their very bones.

As these thoughts were chasing themselves through Harold's mind, the driver restarted the engine and put the car in gear. Now they were travelling cautiously along a road gushing with water and flowing with people. It was as if the cessation of the rain had been an invisible signal. Black people, dressed in bright colours were everywhere, dashing across the road, meandering along the centre of the roadway, walking ankle deep in water at its edge.

Serious thoughts forgotten, Melanie watched, fascinated. Colour shone everywhere. Market stalls awash with vivid-hued swathes of material — home-dyed, home-spun, home-printed, striped, brilliant — plastic bowls, sandals, woven mats, woven hats. There, a stall stacked high with vegetables of deep green, light green, purple, yellow, orange, red. Here, spices smelling strongly enough to make you sneeze: black peppercorns, pink peppercorns, misshapen lumpy ginger roots, bright red chillies, green chillies, a vivid yellow powder, groundnuts in their papery cases. Flowers spilling into strange fruits, some of which she knew — papayas, pineapples, plantains, tiny green bananas.

The car was picking up speed, moving at running

The Lion Mountains

pace. People wherever she looked. Women. Mothers. Half-naked. Small black babies sucking at huge black breasts. Tiny black fists kneading. Bundles of firewood, balanced on heads. More bundles and baskets. All balanced on heads. Children. Wet. Naked. Laughing. Flashing white-toothed smiles. Shacks. Houses. And, illuminating everything, the blazing light of the African sun.

A huge tree.

"Is that the Cotton Tree?" Elizabeth asked suddenly. The street had widened near the museum and the Court House, both splendid colonial buildings. Melanie hastily squirmed round in her seat, craning her neck to see the wide canopy of the tree.

"Yes, mam, dat sure is de Cotton Tree!" It was the driver who replied to the question, his eyes and teeth flashing a smile in the rear view mirror. "And dere is fruit bats livin' in dat tree. Dey is flyin' around at dusk."

Harold squeezed his wife's hand and nodded. He was about to speak when the driver put his foot down and the car accelerated forward. Pedestrians jumped out of the way, but there were no scowls. With distance, the whole tree shrank into view.

"Why is the Cotton Tree so important, Daddy?"

"It's a symbol of freedom and justice, not just to the people who live in Freetown but to all Sierra Leoneans."

"Why?"

"It's a long story, sweetheart, so listen carefully. In the American War of Independence …"

"America?"

"Yes, the British used to rule America but then, in

1775, the Americans rebelled against what they thought were the injustices of The Crown..."

"What Crown?"

"The Crown means the Government of the United Kingdom."

"Our United Kingdom?"

"Yes, England, Scotland ..."

"Wales and Ireland!"

"Northern Ireland," her father corrected. "Now, listen! The American States rebelled against the Crown ..."

"Is that when they dumped all the tea in the harbour at Boston and called it a tea party?" At her father's raised eyebrows she continued: "Mrs Carey told me about it. She was reading a book called...."

"Yes, I'll hear about that later, Melanie. I am telling you the story of the Cotton Tree. In the American War of Independence ..."

"The British lost the War, didn't they?"

"Yes, but before they lost, several runaway and freed slaves had come over to the British side..."

"There were slaves in *America*?"

"Yes, on the cotton fields in the south of the continent and in the sugar plantations in the West Indies, too ... though the sugar plantations were mostly owned by the French and British."

Melanie looked shocked. "My teacher told me America was 'the Land of Opportunity'. I didn't know they have slaves."

"No, sweetheart, they don't have slaves in America any more. I'm talking about nearly two hundred years ago. Then they did have slaves — and a lot of them came over to the British side. Unfortunately, that didn't help the slaves much because the British lost the war. The British had to do something with them, so they arranged for them to be sent to Canada. Nova Scotia, to be exact. Some also went to the West Indies and some to London."

"But what has this to do with The Cotton Tree?"

Harold smiled. "Patience, little one! The freed slaves hated the places they were sent to. They found Canada and London far too cold and they weren't very keen on the other people in the West Indies. They asked to be sent somewhere else and the British listened. They had recently acquired part of the land round here so this is where they were sent, over a thousand of them."

"Were they all in one ship?"

"No, but the ships all arrived here at the same time in about 1794. They needed a place to gather and they saw a huge Cotton Tree — the very same one we passed a little while ago — not far from the sea shore. It was the perfect place, the perfect landmark. So the first thing they did was to hold a service of thanks to God for having their own free land. Then they made their first camp under the tree. Ever since, the Cotton Tree has been a symbol of freedom and democracy."

"That is *ironic*!" Elizabeth muttered under her breath.

"What?" enquired Harold, testily.

"I was reading that Freetown's natural harbour was the centre of the black slave trade."

Shrugging, Harold gave her a rueful smile.

"You're right, of course, darling. It was."

"But I think there's something rather wonderful

about the fact that this was the place where everything changed."

"Not for a while, I suspect. I think the first settlers must have had a very difficult time. But everything changed again in the early nineteenth century when the Slave Trade was abolished in Britain."

Elizabeth's brows drew together in thought. "1807, I think you said?"

"Yes. That date is important to this country. Soon afterwards the British felt so righteous that they established Freetown and its immediate hinterland …"

"What's a hinterland?" Melanie interrupted.

"The land behind the town and the coast." Elizabeth whispered since Harold was now in full flow.

"… Sierra Leone became a British colony the next year. And the British decided to take action to stop all trading in slaves. They had the largest, strongest navy so they could fight slaving ships belonging to any nation and free the slaves. But then they had to find somewhere to take them. The answer was to bring them all to Freetown. About *fifty thousand* of them over the next half century!"

"That was good, wasn't it, Daddy?" Melanie sounded doubtful.

"Good and bad, sweetheart. Good and bad."

"But it was good they had all been freed."

"Yes, but the freed slaves were captives who had been taken from all over Africa. They came from many different tribes and few even spoke the same language. They were just dumped here and told to get on with their lives! It's a beautiful place with the third largest natural harbour in the world, so you can imagine what the native people — the ones who had already lived here for generations — thought of sharing it with foreigners. They were annoyed, very annoyed!"

Here her father paused to light a cigarette. He took a long drag and allowed the thin blue smoke to drift out through his lips before he spoke again.

"Talk about a half-baked idea! There was already rivalry between the many indigenous tribes in this part of Africa. But the British Government thought one black man was the same as another. Never mind their differences! Differences, not only of language, but in their food, their customs, their dress, their buildings. Words fail me! I believe that we have not seen the last of all the unrest in this part of Africa caused by that simple 'expedient'."

"Now, Harold, don't upset yourself," her mother soothed. "The Creoles have been a force for good in Freetown. They learned to live together. They found a common language in English and a common love of Christ and democracy. None of that can be a problem, surely?"

"That worked when the British were here to handle the differences between the various tribes, I grant you that," her husband said grudgingly. "But they've had internal self-government for five years now and everything is falling apart. Now they're pushing for independence from Britain! They'll get it soon, I'm sure. We're giving in to every Tom, Dick and Harry so why not to Sierra Leone, too? But I *really* dread to think what will happen in the future. Civil war, I shouldn't be surprised

…"

"Oh no!" Melanie wailed.

Her mother shot her father a warning glance. "Daddy doesn't mean it, darling. He's just worried about the future. Look at all those smiling people! Do they look as if they're angry? Of course they don't!"

Warned by the sound of chanting, the driver slowed the car to a crawl as they rounded a tight corner. Sure enough, ahead of them, a large party of African women and children were taking up the whole of the road as they danced and sang, the children bouncing up and down, the women's hips swinging from side to side in colourful harmony. Still singing, clapping and swaying, they drew to the side of the road to let the vehicle pass.

A couple of little boys ran along beside the car, trying to race it. Gradually dropping back as it picked up speed, they continued to dance, wide grins shining brightly in their black faces. Melanie saw they were waving at her. As she waved and smiled back she decided they were the very happiest people she had ever seen. Daddy must be wrong, she thought. But Daddy was always right — Mummy had said so and she was always right, too.

- 4 -

RUSSELL LODGE

Melanie suddenly realised that she had not asked a vital question.

"Where are we going, Daddy?"

Her father laughed. "Home!" he said.

"Where's home?"

"Up in the mountains, sweetheart. Not far!"

"How far?"

"A couple of miles, maybe three."

"How soon will we be there?"

Her father turned his wrist, automatically checking the time. "At this rate, Maurice, I reckon another ten minutes at the most?"

"Yessir, boss." The affirmative answer was accompanied by a broad smile.

Steep the mountains were, and she had already noticed how the thunderclouds wrapped their peaks in dark cotton wool before the rain swept down towards the coast. But now the clouds had disappeared and the sun's hot rays were baking the jungle that clothed the precipitous slopes, raising steam that drifted in the slight breeze. Like the autumn mists over the fields of her uncle's farm in Kent, Melanie reminisced. For a moment she allowed herself to think of England and the special cousins she had left there, not to mention her adored elder brother, Trevor, who had almost finished the five years of study at university that would qualify him as a veterinary surgeon. How she would like to share this excitement with them all! Trevor would know all about it of course, but then he knew everything. Anne and Jane were much younger than Trevor, more like sisters than cousins, she knew they would scoff at her attempts at description. Let them, she thought, their eyes would be wide with wonder if they were here. But *they* weren't and *she* was — so she was the luckiest of the three of them to be surrounded by all this strangeness and beauty.

She twisted this way and that trying to see everything as well as where they were heading, but the country road was destined to defeat her efforts. Rising snakelike up the side of the Lion Mountains, the main road was newly surfaced with tarmac and in excellent condition. But on either side raw scars showed where the jungle vegetation had been hacked back and the tracks leading off here and there into the bush were narrow and unpaved. As the road uncoiled in a series of hairpin bends, the car climbed smoothly up the mountain's side. Suddenly the edge of the road seemed to fall away. Melanie looked down into the abyss and saw a clear wide river surging over rocks, funnelling down the valley to empty into the vast expanse of the ocean far below.

"What a huge river!" she remarked, thinking of the narrow lazy Stour that trickled through the English market town of Ashford. This was a river as huge and impressive as the mountains that towered into the clouds, dominating the port's plateau and guarding the entrance to the fertile land that lay beyond them.

"Rivers are called creeks here," her father corrected.

"Why?" she asked.

"Rivers generally run further across country. Creeks are short in length and shallow. Some of these only run with water after a rainstorm, and when they do they run into an inlet — a bay in the coastline."

"Do you mean the sea?"

"Yes, I suppose I do, sweetheart. Depending on the height of the tide, a bay can be deep or shallow. Sometimes fish are left behind by the tide. The natives spear them. They eat a lot of fish here."

The driver had slowed the car to make the right-angled turn onto a bridge. The sound of the tyres on the road changed, as if the wheels were hollow and filled with ball bearings.

Beneath the bridge, water fell in such a sheer, straight drop that one brief glance made Melanie feel dizzy. She hurriedly raised her eyes a fraction, before looking again. The waterfall cascaded into a deep wide pool beside which ran a narrow path. Half hidden by the spray of the gushing torrent, women were busy washing clothes in the crystal-clear cold water of the creek. Their sarongs hitched up to show strong black limbs, they were beating their washing against water-darkened rocks, loosening the dirt into the tumbling waters. A motley collection of coloured clothes was already stretched across boulders to dry in the sunshine: by contrast, Melanie noticed, white garments were draped over bushes.

Before she could ask, her mother supplied the answer to her unspoken question.

"The rocks are hot so coloured clothes dry very

quickly when they're spread out like those. White things are laid on green leaves or grass. Have I ever told you why?" Melanie shook her head. "The gypsies at home in England used to do that. They said it made whites whiter. And they were right, because green leaves use carbon dioxide — the gas we breathe out — and sunshine to make sugar for the plant, and as they do their leaves give off oxygen. Oxygen bleaches — so it makes the clothes whiter. Isn't that clever?"

Melanie thought it was. How surprising that gypsies in England knew this as well as African women. Even the word 'bleach' made her nose wrinkle. She remembered the big plastic bottle of chemical stuff that was kept under the sink in the kitchen. She hated the smell of it but it did make things clean, and it was good for keeping germs away, Mummy said, but you always had to wear rubber gloves when you used it or it would burn your skin. Melanie thought it would be much nicer to use green leaves and sunlight.

As they rounded the next corner, her attention was caught by the sight of an African woman's wide hips swinging up the road in front of the car. Melanie was fascinated by the tribe of small children that surrounded the woman. As far as she could remember, she had never seen anyone walk as they did: barefoot, they moved in an easy, loose-limbed way that was almost like dancing. Their jet-black hair clung to their heads in such tight curls that she was reminded of the rough creamy fleeces of the little lambs she had helped to feed on the farm in England. Briefly, she wondered if it would feel the same as well.

Maurice tooted the horn.

The woman gathered her brood together. With broad sweeps of her arms, she directed them to keep to the side of the road. She was carrying a large bundle on her back and Melanie knew that her father would have said that she was very 'broad in the beam'. As they came closer she made out a small round head and tiny hands sticking out of the bundle and, with a little frisson of shock, she realised it was a baby. But there was an even bigger surprise in store for her as the woman turned to face the vehicle smiling broadly and waving. Melanie had already become used to this greeting but she suddenly realised that the woman was naked from the waist up. One huge pendulous breast swung down past her waist: the other had been tossed over her shoulder to the baby. And sure enough, the baby was suckling, his little fists kneading the breast for all they were worth.

Melanie's eyes grew wide as saucers, and her parents exchanged a smile at her amazement.

The rest of the journey passed quickly and soon the road widened and flattened as, on either side, the ground had been levelled and new concrete houses rose like plants from the red earth. Only they weren't like plants. They were ugly and solid and whitish grey and they didn't belong here, in this fascinating untamed and untameable land. Melanie wanted to cry at the sight of the poor earth all cut and scraped like a grazed knee. Why, it even *looked* as though it was bleeding — red soil and black rocks sticking up like broken bones and blood from the jungle-cleared ground. She knew how much a graze *hurt* and her heart ached for the soil. She wanted more than anything to go and pat it until it felt better, but she knew that she was just being silly.

The driver slowed the car, braked hard and made a sharp right turn into the drive of one of the new houses.

"Here we are, at last! Welcome to your new home, my darlings!" The look in her father's eye and the delight in his voice showed Melanie how proud and happy he was to have found them such a wonderful place to live. So she smiled and took his proffered hand as she jumped down from the rear passenger seat.

But deep inside, a little part of her heart was still weeping for the damage that had been done to the land.

The house that Harold Russell had rented in readiness for the arrival of his wife and youngest child was one of six recently erected, on a site acquired by the civil engineering company for which he worked, to provide home comforts for the more senior of their employees. As Chief Resident Engineer in overall charge and with responsibility for the whole of the river reversal project, he had been entitled to first choice, and had selected the one with the most beautiful view.

Pristine jungle, untouched by human habitation, bordered the property on two sides. Directly in front of the house ran the new road, while to the right the tree-clad land dropped away towards the shore of the Atlantic Ocean. Each evening wide open skies turned red, crimson and carmine as the sun slid slowly into her watery couch, the flames of her demise slowly fading to apricot, peach, and soft salmon pink. Each morning the fiery glow of dawn scattered her rays over the mountain's peak, polishing the jungle leaves with translucency as birds sang and jarred and celebrated her rising. Long shadows shortened as the sky lightened from the East, casting a pale pellucid presence across the wave-flecked surface of the sea. From the shore far below would rise the softened sea-shell sound of lacy-edged waves sluicing the sandy shore, while a diaphanous breeze kissed the land awake.

The house, christened Russell Lodge by its first occupant, had been the first erected on the site. Consequently, the land's sheer exuberance, aided by the warm humid climate, had already softened the harshness of its construction, for a green bloom of growth hid the rawness of red earth.

The house itself was more functional than beautiful, but it contained all the most modern conveniences which could be found in this part of the world and Melanie was much taken with her bedroom with its adjoining dressing-cum-bathroom and narrow balcony. Her parents' bedroom was equipped with more sophisticated conveniences including a wide balcony and a huge built-in wardrobe.

Because the Chief Resident Engineer and his wife were required to offer hospitality to all the prominent members of the community as well as any important executives of the company who visited the country, the downstairs rooms were large and spacious. Harold had arranged for them to be sufficiently furnished for his family's basic needs but he was relying on his wife to supply soft furnishings and all the little details that would turn this basic living space into a home. Elizabeth was itching to begin.

First, however, she was called upon to inspect the kitchen. Built a little to the north of the house itself, the kitchen and scullery were under the aegis of the cook, a fat unpleasant sneering fellow with a grand sense of self-importance. He and his small brow-beaten wife occupied the largest of the buildings in the servants' compound, which, with the kitchen, were divided off from the house and garden by a palisade.

The tour of the kitchen was not a success. Elizabeth was horrified by the evident lack of hygiene. However, she was prepared to begin by giving Cook the benefit of the doubt, deciding that the proof of the pudding would be in the eating. If the food prepared by Cook was palatable that would be a good start, and propitious for the future.

Needing a cook, Harold had accepted the person recommended to him by his foreman. Unfortunately, he had disliked Cook from the first, although the man had flaunted flattering references from previous employers. Harold had a sneaking suspicion that they might have been copied or forged, but, since he worked long hours, he was seldom home and all he had needed until his family arrived had been something to eat and somewhere to sleep. Cook's wife did what cleaning and washing was required while, unknown to Harold, Cook looked on and directed from the master's own chair in the sitting room.

Now he could see that Elizabeth was neither enamoured nor accepting of these arrangements. She looked at Cook with barely concealed disdain but at his wife with considerably more sympathy. Having accompanied her husband around the world from contract to contract, Elizabeth had a wealth of experience in employing servants, and she would have much preferred Harold to have left the choice of all the servants to her. But she realised that, in Cook's eyes, she was the interloper. Nonetheless, she already felt the weight of Cook's disapproval, having quickly discerned that he regarded her with ill-concealed dislike.

She suspected that Harold's meals had consisted mostly of whisky and cigarettes and that the servants had lived well at his expense. Well, that was going to change, she resolved, and it would change fast, now that she was here to take care of her husband as he deserved.

Melanie, on the other hand, danced around the house, the garden and the compound with a child's undisguised glee in her new surroundings, especially when she discovered the bantam hens that Cook's wife had been given leave to keep in the compound. Mrs Cook had given her a shy smile and beckoned her towards the little thatched henhouse. Melanie had to stoop down to look inside and was thrilled to see that one of the hens was sitting on a nest. Elizabeth smiled to see how well the child and the adult communicated despite the lack of a common language. Cook spoke some pidgin English but had forbidden his wife to speak anything other than her native African tongue. However, within a few minutes Melanie was able to tell her mother that the bantam was sitting on four eggs and that they were likely to hatch very soon, possibly that very day.

As they entered the dining room a cloud of flies rose from the dining table where plates of fruit and cheese had been set out, together with a loaf of mouldy grey-brown bread. A large pat of butter stood in its own little circle of grease, the rancid smell of which permeated the room. Flies continued to buzz round the food. Elizabeth was horrified.

"Have you been actually been eating this stuff, Harold?" she cried in dismay. "No wonder you've had a gippy tummy!"

Melanie's father looked both hurt and defiant.

"Just a snack to welcome you," he said. "There'll be curry and rice for dinner later."

"This place is filthy!" Elizabeth declared, picking up plate after plate already smeared with greasy fingerprints. "Take your hand away from that bread, Melanie! Do we have a houseboy, Harold? Or is all this Cook's doing?"

"I thought I'd leave you to appoint the other servants," Harold said meekly.

"Oh, I shall! Indeed I shall. But first I'm going to inspect Cook's cooking pans!" And with those words she flounced out of the room. Melanie was hungry but she knew better than to follow her mother when she was in high dudgeon, so she resorted to sucking her thumb and twisting a lock of hair round her index finger.

"Never mind, sweetheart, Mummy will soon sort everything out. Come here." Her father had thrown himself into an easy chair in the adjoining lounge. "I expect you're hungry," he remarked and a bar of chocolate appeared magically in his hand. "Here's something to keep the wolf from the door."

"Thank you, Daddy," Melanie said politely as she

seized the chocolate from him, wondering whether it was all for her or whether she should share it with him. She did not have to ask.

"Let's take a turn round the garden together. I need a cigarette. And you won't drop chocolate crumbs on the floor if you eat it outside."

Together they went through the open fly door and out into the garden. Indoors, the room had been hot and humid, but outside it was cooler, a slight breeze bearing the fragrance of greenery, the warmth of the earth and the sharp tang of petrol. From the direction of the compound came her mother's firm voice interspersed with the blustering pidgin English of Cook. Even from this distance, Melanie could feel his annoyance and somehow she realised that it was beneath his dignity to receive instructions from a woman, let alone to be reprimanded by one.

"What will happen, Daddy?" she asked.

Her father answered lightly, as if there were no contretemps taking place in the servants' compound. "Mummy will make her views known. Then she will use her charm as well as her authority and the whole household will run like clockwork."

"But I don't think Cook likes Mummy, you know."

Her father sighed. "Unfortunately, Africans have their own ways of doing things and they don't like change. They particularly dislike white men telling them what to do, and as for white women … well, let's just say some have a very poor opinion of white women."

Instead of reassuring her as he intended, her father's words made Melanie anxious. When they had been in

India, less than a year ago, her adored mother had been very ill for a long time. Before they had left England again a week or so previously, Melanie had overheard a conversation between her mother and her aunt. From it, she had gleaned that Elizabeth had almost died before the surgical operation from which she had still not completely recovered, so the little girl was well aware that her mother was not physically strong, although Daddy always said she had the courage of a lion and the tenacity of a python. The child shivered, remembering the time that a python had slithered into their garden in Karachi. She had not realised that such a big snake could move so quickly:

"Keep away, Missy, keep away!" The snake's keeper had rushed into the garden and almost hurled her aside. "Big snake very hungry. He not eating for month. He wanting food now."

Her mother had bustled outside and taken Melanie upstairs to the verandah from where they could look down on the havoc the snake was causing in the flowerbeds, as it searched for small mammals on which to slake its hunger. Eventually, with the aid of a live rat, its keeper had managed to tempt it away from the garden and back along the road. The gardener had been very annoyed: the snake had caused considerable damage to the dahlias that Sahib loved, for they never recovered.

"What did it want, Mummy?" Melanie had asked, and her mother had explained that, in its natural habitat, the immense snake would have a huge meal, perhaps a whole goat, and then it would go to sleep for a long time while it digested its food. A week or two, sometimes a whole month, would pass before the snake felt sufficiently hungry to feed again. This capacity was put to good use by some entrepreneurial local people: they would starve the huge snakes and then hire them out to people or businesses who were having trouble with vermin. A hungry python would make short shrift of rats and mice, perhaps even the occasional mongoose. She carefully made no mention of the fact that they had also been known to prey on cats, dogs and children.

Recalling the python now, Melanie wondered aloud whether there were any snakes in Sierra Leone. Her mother had told her that there were — and that she should be very careful to keep away from them because, although snakes generally slithered away from humans in fright, there were some kinds that preferred to bite and those were the ones that were mortally poisonous. Her father was lighting a cigarette and didn't reply straight away. He sucked the smoke right down to his lungs and let it out slowly, concentrating on blowing smoke rings towards her.

"Yes, there are snakes, most of them poisonous. If you see one, leave it well alone and call me or Mummy or one of the servants. You have to kill them quickly by hitting them hard just behind the head. If you miss they are inclined to bite!" He chuckled, but Melanie didn't think it would be at all funny to be bitten by a mortally poisonous snake. And she didn't like the idea of killing a snake for no reason. She remembered her Indian ayah, Lakshmi, suggesting that she should walk heavily if she saw a snake, explaining that most of the deaf reptiles would feel the vibration and slip away from her. Melanie decided it would be best to stamp everywhere she walked in Sierra Leone — just in case there was a snake nearby.

She was about to say so, when her mother came out from the servants' quarters, saw her husband and daughter in conversation and walked towards them. She looked tired and shaky, and very, very cross.

Just at that moment there came a "Halloo!" from across the road and a tall thin white man dressed in shorts, long socks and a white short-sleeved shirt, came down the drive towards the house. Her father introduced him as his subordinate, Mr Watson, who had arrived a month earlier with his family.

They all shook hands and made the usual enquiries after each others health.

"We feel like old Africa hands now," Simon Watson assured them, "My wife would very much like to meet you and she has insisted I invite you all to dinner tonight. Provided you are not too tired after your journey, Mrs Russell?"

"Oh no! We're too excited to be tired, aren't we Melanie? And shipboard life is so easy. We've been thoroughly spoiled for the last ten days. Thank you, and please thank your wife, too. We'd be delighted to accept such a thoughtful invitation."

"That's settled, then. Shall we say six o'clock?"

Melanie watched as, once again, the adults shook hands and exchanged thanks and good wishes.

She noticed that her mother looked much relieved. "What a kind invitation," Elizabeth said, looking up at her husband from under her eye-lashes. Melanie recognised that look: it meant trouble for someone and it wasn't long before she knew who that particular someone was. "That solves tonight's problem very well indeed. But tomorrow the cook and I are going to clean the whole kitchen from top to bottom! I have never seen such a disgracefully unhygienic place for preparing food. I will need to go to the market myself. And Harold, we need to engage a houseboy before the end of tomorrow. Or I shall be on the first plane back to England."

Despite these brave words, Melanie could see that her mother was exhausted. She would need a lot of help. Well, Melanie thought, I am nearly a whole year older now, and I've grown a lot as well. I'm the one to help Mummy sort out this problem with the servants.

On balance, the welcome dinner was a success. Mrs Watson had obviously been very nervous: but then she hardly knew her husband's superior, let alone his newly arrived wife and small daughter. Elizabeth understood her hostess's nervousness, not having forgotten her own debut as a colonial dinner party hostess in Burma before the War. West Africa was new to her, too, for although Sierra Leone had been a British colony for two hundred years, it had been only recently that British engineering companies had felt sufficiently reassured of the country's stability to be prepared to invest in its infrastructure. The project on which her husband was working was ambitious: to change the flow of a large river so that, instead of plunging quickly into the sea, it would irrigate the fertile land behind the mountains.

Elizabeth, seeing her husband was sharing an anecdote with his hostess, quietly asked her host how much he was enjoying his work?

"I'm honoured to be working under your husband, Mrs Russell," he responded. "He has such a wealth of knowledge and experience yet he is prepared to trust and encourage a mere stripling like me. He is even prepared to listen to my suggestions. However, I'm aware that he finds the laissez-faire, 'tomorrow will do', attitude of the local labourers a bit trying."

"I am sure everyone will know if he finds *anything* trying," Elizabeth remarked dryly, before adding: "But it's an interesting project, I believe? A far cry from constructing the usual roads and storage tanks?"

Mr Watson grinned. "Yes, I must admit, it's not often that we reverse the direction of flow of a whole river by tunnelling through a mountain! You must come out to the site, Mrs Russell. I'm sure you'll find it interesting — and, if, as I presume, your husband is too heavily involved to be able to show you around, I would be delighted to do so myself."

"Thank you," Elizabeth said lightly, "I may well take you up on your offer."

Melanie had been concentrating all evening on behaving well and had kept very quiet, but she was feeling very tired after all the excitement of the day. Feeling her eyes closing of their own accord, she forced them open and quietly placed her napkin beside her plate.

"Please may I get down?"

The conversation stopped abruptly. Four pairs of adult eyes turned towards her. They had clearly almost forgotten she was there. It was seldom that a child was invited to dinner in the evening. High tea at five o'clock in the afternoon (or sometimes earlier) was usually a child's lot, so that they could be put to bed before the evening frivolities began. But, in view of the problem with Cook, Melanie had been invited to this dinner while the Watson's two little children had been safely tucked up in bed.

"Have you had enough, Melanie?"

"Yes, thank you, Mrs Watson. I have had ample."

Elizabeth understood how exhausted the little girl was. She glanced at her husband. At his almost imperceptible nod, she said: "Of course, darling, I'm sure Mr and Mrs Watson won't mind if you go and sit in the sitting room."

As Melanie slid down from her chair, Elizabeth turned to her hostess. "Thank you very much for your very timely invitation, Emily. It has been such a pleasure to meet you. And the food has been delicious. You are indeed fortunate in your cook. Which reminds me, how does one go about finding a houseboy? Harold has not needed one while he has been here on his own, you see, but I'm sure we will now."

Emily Watson smiled. "I must admit that I have no idea, Elizabeth. My husband arranged everything before I came out, but I'm sure our servants will have some family member to recommend. When are you interviewing?"

"I was hoping to appoint someone tomorrow, if at all possible. Melanie is only staying out here with us during her summer holidays, so she will be returning to England in a couple of months. Of course, I would very much like to spend as much time with her as I can."

The Melanie concerned was sitting sleepily on the sofa within earshot, swinging her legs to and fro in an effort to stay awake, but she noticed the look that passed between the houseboy and the cook who was overseeing the service from the kitchen corridor.

"Talking of Melanie, I know she is exhausted after the excitement of the day and I'm sure you must both be very frazzled by having to put on dinner — and what a splendid one it was! — at such short notice. I expect your little ones are up early in the morning, too." She laid her own napkin down and rose from her seat. "So, if you will excuse us, Melanie and I will take our leave."

"Of course," Mr Watson leapt to his feet. "I will accompany you. It's pitch black outside until the moon rises. I'll bring a torch."

"I'll follow shortly, darling. This whisky is too good to hurry."

And you're enjoying the attention of a pretty young woman, Elizabeth thought indulgently. But I am exhausted and I shall be glad to sleep in a proper bed tonight.

She bid her hosts a grateful 'Goodnight', took Melanie's hand and allowed the two of them to be escorted over the road and down the drive to the front door of their new home.

Melanie had not realised how different darkness can feel in a hot and humid place — as though someone had thrown a steaming towel over you after you'd just stepped out of the bath. The black velvet night hung like a dense curtain around them and yet it was alive with movement and strange half-sounds from the jungle. The drip of moisture, the sound of tiny scurrying feet, the rustle of leaves, all contributed to the busy disquiet of the night. She felt the passage of something flying overhead, a subtle change in the air pressure of the velvet dark, a skimming slightness of breeze. She clung tightly to her mother's hand, her eyes wide-staring, willing herself to see what moved. A finger of moonlight rose above the jungled mountainside, momentarily stilling all movement and casting pale eerie shadows over the scene ahead. In the distance, the almost motionless water of the cape glimmered. In that sheen of silver, something flew swiftly, noiselessly ... and very close.

"Oh, bats!" Her mother let her breath out in a sibilant hiss that was half relieved sigh and half surprise. As if to tease them, bats flew silently back and forth across the moon's glistening reflection. Fearing the creatures would become snarled in her hair, Melanie urged her mother onwards by tugging at her hand. It was only when the door was safely closed behind them that she allowed herself to breathe, her breath like a live thing in her chest and her heart-beat pounding in her ears.

Over time, she would become accustomed to the strange restiveness of tropical nights. She learned of the many species that, hiding from the sun in the daytime, rapidly appeared as soon as cool darkness fell to temper the scalding heat of day; for night's swift fall was the signal for insects, mammals and reptiles to creep out of their daytime resting place to forage for food in the coolness of the dying day.

Unlike the slow English dusk that gradually eased the

eyes from light to dark, here blackness fell suddenly as soon as the sun was lost beneath the ocean's horizon. Melanie thought it was like a musical she had once seen at the theatre: one moment the sunlight was dancing joyously on the stage, and the next, night's thick curtain had fallen to hide the stage and its players from view.

In time she would come to treasure the bats' flight, their smooth, soft, slinkiness enlivening the instant transition of day to night. But tonight, as she sleepily climbed the stairs to her bedroom, she was too tired to wonder about anything — let alone about the nature of the mysterious country in which she now found herself.

- 5 -
JUNGLE

Despite her misgivings, Melanie slept. In her dreams bats wove through long bending fronds, beneath which strange blossoms bloomed, their fragrance perfuming the balmy night with a lush richness that reminded her of jasmine and rotting apples, with a hint of silage. Pervasive and heady, the smell spoke to her of life's bounty in the midst of death: the odour of the jungle where life's full cycle was unstayed by the civilising hand of man. She felt her heart respond to the primordial vibration that was all around her. Beams of moonlight parted the darkness, striking silver flashes from leaves; stems swaying in the windless quiet of the night. And all around, in moonlight and shadow, water made its presence felt: in the warm humidity of blossoms' breath; in small sweet pools gathering drop by drop in the hollow palms of huge leaves; in the sweaty puddles beneath the undergrowth from which insects rose in clouds; in the soft murmurings of running water; in the gurgling meanderings of small streams. Water dropping precipitously into thirsty creeks and shimmering between the black wedges of their banks.

Through her whole being ran the thrumming drum beat of Africa. The land itself was claiming her for its own, holding her to its breast. Bound to the continent's vastness, she felt her own smallness. Like the baby she had seen bound to his mother's back, she blended into the Earth Mother's bountiful presence, aware that all her needs, and more, would be supplied. She saw again the child sucking at his mother's breast and knew deep in her core that she too was a child of this ancient nurturer, whose hot damp breath beaded on her pale skin. In her dream, she stepped into Africa's luxuriant shadows and her skin grew black and beautiful, rich and shining with the essence of life. And through it all the deep, dark drumbeat of the Earth's heart, shuddered through her body, drawing her in … drawing her in … until she felt herself becoming … becoming … becoming … the beat itself. As the rhythm of life drew her into the heart of Africa, the drum beat faded and she slipped into a deep, slow-breathing sleep.

She woke refreshed, wondering where she was. Sunlight sliced through a gap in the curtains, bright and hot. No motion. She was not on the ship, then. No, of course not! She remembered now. How could she have forgotten? She threw open the curtains and the heat of morning flowed through her as she gazed out onto the shimmering blue of the distant ocean.

Outside was the world she had seen yesterday, but it might just as well have been a thousand years ago. I was looking in then, Melanie thought — and the thought was peculiar but true. Now I'm looking out. Now I am not only *in* Africa, I am *of* Africa. It was not a thought, she realised, it was an owning of the truth. She wanted to run to her parents and to yell: "I am not in Africa, I am of Africa!" But she knew it was a truth that she could not express. It was her truth, not theirs. Rocking backwards and forwards in delight, she hugged the warm feeling to herself, her smile as broad as an African's, her heart as big and commodious as the continent itself. She felt the richness of her soul.

But she could not express these things. Her thoughts were confused. Action was required. She quickly dressed, paid lip service to the toothbrush and dragged a hairbrush once only through her curls. Slipping quietly down the stairs, she found the front door unlocked and let herself out into the garden. She stopped abruptly. All along the drive, flowing out into the road, were people: all of them black, mostly men, some squatting, some standing, some old and grizzled of head, some young and straight. Fat, thin, tall, short, some with their mothers, others holding a child by the hand, they waited. Silently. Patiently. Melanie found herself staring open mouthed. Then, realising it was rude to stare so, she hurriedly backed into the house. She fled up the stairs.

"Mummy! Daddy! Look out of the window! You must get up! You must come!"

She rounded the door into her parents room to find that they were both awake. Her father was standing beside the bed adjusting the knot in the front of his 'Shan bombies', the wide cotton trousers that he habitually wore for sleeping. Her mother was sitting up in bed, her hand hiding the last vestiges of an enormous yawn.

"What is it, darling?" she enquired as soon as her lips came together again, but it was her husband who answered as he twitched the curtain back from the window.

"I see the bush telegraph has been working overtime," he said. "There must be at least twenty."

"Twenty what?" Elizabeth was pulling her housecoat on over her flimsy nightdress. On reaching his side, she peered out of the window, discreetly using the curtain to disguise her state of undress. "Oh! My!"

"Don't worry, my darling," Harold said smugly. "You get dressed and I'll go and sort the sheep from the goats."

"You'll do no such thing!" his wife snapped. "If you could engage a cook who hasn't the faintest idea of cleanliness, I dread to think who you would choose as a houseboy." She softened the words with a smile, heading into the bathroom as she spoke, fresh clothes laid over her arm. "But I would appreciate it if you would tell them that I will be down directly."

"Come on, sweetheart." Her father held out his hand to Melanie. "Let's do as your mother asks."

Half an hour later, Elizabeth was ensconced at the head of the dining table with a note pad in front of her. She scribbled notes as each applicant vacated the interviewee's chair she had set to the right of the table, facing her. Melanie, seated beside her mother, was engaged in busily drawing some of the images from her dreams of the previous night, when something about the man who had just seated himself across from her, caught her attention.

He was short, muscular and very dark, with fuzzy black hair lying close to his head in looser curls than most of the men she'd seen that morning, but his most obvious feature was a long twisted scar that ran down the left side of his face, from temple to mouth, pulling up his lip in a sneer. His eyes met hers and instead of smiling like the others, he scowled and dropped his eyes. Melanie, repulsed but fascinated by his face, sat very still and tried not to breathe, scared that he would look at her — for something in his glance made her shiver.

His resentful gaze stirred up memories. Melanie found herself remembering how the hotel doorman would shoo away the frighteningly disfigured beggars who used to congregate outside the Taj Mahal Hotel in Bombay. Within minutes they would return, hands like claws upturned, begging for arms in a high sing-song voice. Eventually the doorman would become so incensed that he would call the police. At the sound of the police vehicle's siren, the beggars would melt away into the crowded street and disappear for perhaps half an hour.

No-one could help but be horrified by the dreadful disfigurements borne by the beggars. Many had no arms, or no hands, or no ears, or a slit nose and one bulging sightless eye. These she remembered with repugnance and pity. Her heart wept for them and she would always twitch at her mother's skirt asking for an anna or two to give them, despite the fact that she knew that to give anything to one of them would bring a horde of others, buzzing like flies round a rotting carcass.

She remembered the Beggar King in particular. He was all the more frightening because his face was at the same level as hers. He sat on his platform with wheels, the place on which he lived his whole life. His severe disabilities — he had no legs, a stump for an arm, his nose appeared to have been gnawed by rats and he had only one hand, the other being shrivelled into a rat-like paw — were terrible. In fact, his whole face was twisted, but it was the avaricious, malevolent glint in his eye that most horrified her. Once she had overheard a conversation amongst the adults from which she learned, to her horror, that it was often the impoverished parents of a child who, seeing no future for their offspring other than death, would purposefully deform it soon after birth, by removing limbs or eyes or tongue, so that the child should always have an opportunity to survive — as a beggar.

For nights after seeing the Beggar King she would have nightmares. Nightmares in which he raced after her on his string-guided cart, gaining on her until his malevolent yellow eyes were an inch from hers and the putrid decay on his breath was all she could smell. His hand would graze against her shoulder and she would wake soaking in sweat, to find her ayah gently holding her down in the bed with one hand, stroking her brow with the other and whispering calming Hindi-sweet words in her ear. Melanie had been told that she had suffered a very high fever for over a week and that Lakshmi had nursed her day and night until she was well.

How she missed Lakshmi now! At first, she had not wanted an ayah, but Lakshmi had been much more to her than a nursemaid. She hoped that Lakshmi was better now. Melanie always remembered her in the 'God-blesses' after the Lord's Prayer, and she would often recall the calm gentleness of her face the last time she had seen her, asleep in the shade of the jacaranda tree. But when she mentioned Lakshmi to her mother, Elizabeth would smile sadly and say she was sure she was well again now. Melanie had already learned to distrust the things that adults said when they wanted you to think something that wasn't quite true: she was aware that they wished her to be happy and not sad, but sometimes it was better to know the truth, even if it hurt.

Besides, only the other night she had dreamed of Lakshmi. They were running together towards the elephants' enclosure in the Hanging Gardens on Bombay's Malabar Hill where Nelly, the baby elephant, was waiting for them. Lakshmi was running fast and freely, smiling and laughing and chatting in high-pitched Hindi which, Melanie now realised, *she had understood*. The little girl had known then that old Lakshmi was dead and that she would never find her ayah again even if she went back to Bombay when she was grown up, and searched and searched.

Her mother was still interviewing the scarred man; he was replying with a weird lop-sided grimace that she realised was a smile. Slowly, so as not to be seen, she slid down from her chair. Softly she stole from the room and out of the back door. Looking to her left, towards the jungle, she saw the swing her father had put up for her hanging from the branch of a huge cotton tree. Soon she was swinging back and forth, back and forth, mesmerised by the motion.

She banished the Beggar King from her memory, together with Lakshmi — but the face of the scarred man would not leave her mind. How, she asked herself, had he been injured so badly? Had his parents disfigured him because they were poor, like some poverty-stricken people did in India? Had he been fighting? Some of the other men had scars on their bodies, but they looked as if they were *meant* to be there. The scars formed patterns and some had little raised ridges of skin like beads, set at intervals in the designs. Melanie thought they were curious and, while she didn't like them, she could see that they were interesting. Which brought her back to the man Mummy was interviewing: his scar had a violence to it that made him very ugly, as well as frightening and a little bit terrifying to look at — so you didn't want to look but couldn't quite help it. And all the while she felt his pain tapping into some long-forgotten race memory within her.

Slowly, slowly, she let herself be lulled by the swing's repetitive motion until she ceased to think. Although her mind was stilled, her eyes were fixed on the vivid green shimmering leaves of the jungle. It was as if they were moving and not her. Back and forth, back and forth she swung. The leaves stirred and the greenness called to her with its song of coolness and shade, of dappled light dancing with gloom, of blossom amongst dense vegetation, of moss, water and huge tree-like ferns. The jungle's ancient magic, its primordial smell, the thrill of its unknown dangers, all reached out to enfold her. A fragrance redolent of spices enticed her, beckoning her into its warm, humid embrace.

Melanie allowed herself to slip from the swing's seat to her feet — feet that took her, unheeding, closer to the edge of the jungle. Just a little way, she thought. I might find a treasure like gold or diamonds or orchids or a multi-coloured feather. Only a little way, just to feel the coolness. She scratched her arm where points of prickly heat were beginning to rise. It's so hot and humid here in the garden, even swinging backwards and forwards the air is hot on my face. In the jungle it will be cool and quiet. The chattering people in the lessening queue nearby were speaking faster and more loudly. Her head was beginning to ache. So noisy. So hot. So sweaty.

Melanie knew that if her own head was feeling too big and about to burst, then Mummy must be about to get one of her migraines when her head hurt so much that she had to lie in a darkened room. Sometimes she was there for what seemed like days and days until she was very sick, after which the headache would slowly get better and Mummy would eventually come downstairs looking pale and thin and wobbly. For days she would wear her dark glasses indoors as well as out and Melanie would see how difficult it was for her to turn her head or even to smile.

I know! She thought, I'll pick some wild flowers for Mummy. She loves wild flowers. Melanie smiled to remember her mother telling her that one day God had taken his watercolours and a large brush and washed the whole earth in blue for the sky and the sea, and green for the forests and jungles — and the fields and meadows, of course. And then he stood back and looked and thought it needed a little yellow ochre for the desert, and red and brown for the earth when it was ploughed. But it still wasn't colourful enough, so he took his finest sable hair paint brush and added little points and flecks of colour: vermillion and scarlet and mauve and purple and white and bright, bright blue like forget-me-nots and daffodil yellow and white for the wonderful Rose of Sharon that turns pink at noon and crimson in the evening and … and … and … Yes! She saw a crimson flower beckoning to her from the dense foliage that surrounded the garden.

I'll stamp all the way, Melanie thought, suiting the action to the words. Snakes and wild creatures will run away. She picked the beautiful flower and sniffed. Its stamens left a golden tinge on her nose but its beautiful petals offered no fragrance. Disappointed, she ventured a little further into the greenness, hoping to find more satisfactory flowers. She heard the high-pitched whine of a mosquito … and another … and another. Flying insects were all around. Biting her. Drawing blood.

She found herself spinning, trying to find a way out of the dense foliage that had become her cage. Her foot caught. She fell headlong to the jungle floor, scraping her elbow and knees. The insects descended on her cuts. Too frightened to cry, paralysed with fear, she froze, her breath fast and uneven. A sinewy slithery movement close by, only just discernible through the needling whining mist of insects. Blood roared in her ears. She turned her head. No movement. Then her eyes made out a huge snake, slowly but inexorably sliding down a branch only a few inches from where she lay. The snake stilled, raised its head and tasted the air with its forked tongue. Its head darted forward. Melanie was on her feet and running, blundering forwards, parting vines, pushing through leaves and stems and fronds and wild willowy jungle things, desperately seeking the sunlight of the garden. And wishing so much to be the meek,

The Lion Mountains

compliant, obedient little girl on the swing.

I'm stupid, stupid, stupid, she thought, as tears of fear and frustration began to course down her cheeks. The jungle was against her now! She felt its power and its malevolence enveloping her, trapping her. Smells deepened, became unbearably dank, unendurably dark, insufferably unwholesome. She smelled the snake-smell around her, its heavy stink reminding her of the farm's slurry pit. Now she could almost hear its hissing breath close to her ear. Perhaps African snakes ate bigger things than mice and rats and the occasional mongoose, she thought in terror.

Something seemed to be running behind her. She stopped. The jungle behind her stirred and was still. Her heart missed a beat as she remembered: she was in the Lion Mountains! Perhaps the thing behind her was a lion? Yes, it must be! Lions definitely liked to eat little girls. Cautiously, she started on again. Stopped. Remembered. Lions stalked their prey. Then they pounced suddenly. Like the farm cat when he killed a rat. Hardly daring to breathe, she crept onwards, eyes wide and staring. Looking fearfully from side to side while her heart played a timpani in her chest.

Somewhere beneath her panic she remembered her father telling her an anecdote about being chased by a lion: the moral was 'if anything is chasing you, stay absolutely still.' Again, she froze. Her bites were tingling and her nose was itching ready to sneeze, but she must stay quite still until the lion moved away. She felt its concealed lion eyes glaring at her. Its lips drawn back. Its teeth bared in a silent snarl. She could feel it crouching close by, behind a huge green jungle leaf. Ready to spring.

The leaf trembled. She must stay still. The lion would sense movement. Any movement at all. But the sneeze was creeping down her nose ... further ... she mustn't even sniff ... further ... no, please ... no ...

A-TISH-OOO ! She sneezed.

Large warm hands grabbed her from behind, plucked her up and she found herself being purposefully carried at silent speed. Too shocked to protest, she looked up into a black face, young, handsome and very fierce. The man's full pouted lips were tightly closed, his eyes fixed ahead, yet she could feel the tense alertness within him and knew better than to utter a word. Instead she clung to him, tears streaking down her cheeks. Where was he taking her? Was he saving her? Or were they going deeper and deeper into the jungle? She had no way of knowing. Was he taking her for a slave? Did people still take slaves in Africa? Did they like little white girls for slaves, *particularly*?

The panic started to subside. The man's body was sleek and warm against her skin. And he smelled warm, too, with another richer smell beneath the warmth like garlicky goat. Whoever this stranger was who had found her, at least she wasn't being eaten alive by a snake or a lion.

The green gloom ended abruptly. The man stepped out into the sunlight and set her down on her feet. She looked round wildly. There was the swing, her swing. And there was Mummy rushing towards her, arms outstretched. As her mother fell to her knees Melanie flew headlong into her arms, sobbing with relief and joy. Her mother kissed her and hugged her and told her that she had been very naughty indeed and very, very disobedient.

Melanie said she had only wanted to pick some pretty flowers for Mummy because she knew she would have a headache after all the work she was doing, and she had only found one and here it was, still in her hand, and she held it out all crushed and battered as it was. And her mother took it and pressed it to her cheek and said it was beautiful but that if Melanie ever went into the jungle again she would definitely smack her very hard indeed. But she was half smiling and half crying as she said it, so Melanie knew she didn't really mean it.

It seemed a good time to tell her mother that her insect bites were beginning to *really hurt*, not just itch, so she did. And her mother said she must have a lukewarm bath with some of Mummy's own special oil in it, and then she would make sure that every single bite was covered in calamine lotion and wouldn't Melanie look funny all daubed with white patches, like the spotted cow on the farm? Only Melanie said that the cow had black splotches on white skin and hers would be the other way around, and her mother laughed and hugged her even more tightly.

Then she asked who it was who had found her and her mother looked shocked and said: 'Oh! How could I have forgotten to thank him? Where has he gone?' But there was no-one to be seen in the garden. Her saviour had completely disappeared. Melanie imagined he might have disappeared in a puff of smoke like the genie in

Aladdin, but her mother said no, he was a real young man, and she would find him even if it was the last thing she did, so that Melanie could thank him personally.

And then her mother took Melanie up the stairs and ran the bath and did all the things she had promised. Afterwards, her skin was all patchy with calamine lotion, but she didn't mind even though she did look like the spotted cow in reverse.

So much happened during the next week that Melanie felt she must be much older than when she had arrived.

She was glad it was only a week because she loved beautiful Sierra Leone and wanted to stay as long as possible and now seven whole weeks still remained before she had to fly back to school in England. Her mother had told her this and had added that she was a very lucky girl because most schoolgirls only had six weeks' summer holiday in total and she had already enjoyed a school-free fortnight on the ship to Africa.

As her father had predicted, by the end of the first week of her mother taking control, the household had settled down into an apparently harmonious pattern.

Elizabeth had thrown up her hands in horror when she saw the state of the kitchen. Her first self-appointed task had been to oversee the kitchen being well and truly scrubbed by Cook's wife, the man himself being above such menial tasks. She had decided to tackle his overweening importance gradually, rather than to tackle him head-on. So she merely made her presence felt by dropping by to inspect as each cleaning task was completed. The kitchen walls and floors were scrubbed;

the utensils inspected, scoured if redeemable and replaced if not; all stores were inspected and most tossed out.

Although he had boasted of his knowledge about modern European methods of storing food, Cook had not used the refrigerator. Instead, traditional pottery crocks had been employed, allowing huge cockroaches to proliferate. Nor had he set any value on the new cooker, preferring to use an open fire which he had built in the centre of the floor. Over this, suspended from a tripod, hung a blackened pot, always full of curry, although the actual ingredients of the curry were impossible to distinguish. The sink appeared to have been used for purposes other than those acceptable in European kitchens. Elizabeth had closed her eyes to what those uses had probably been, preferring blissful ignorance, but had overseen its thorough cleanse. She supplied several large bottles of bleach for the disinfection of the whole kitchen in general and the sink in particular.

Elizabeth suspected that the rest of the servants' compound was similarly dirty and would need her attentions in due course, but, to begin with, she concentrated on the cleanliness of the kitchen, making it abundantly clear to Cook that that unless he complied with her edicts on hygiene he would be summarily dismissed.

She tried to tread gently so as not to destroy the man's pride, but she knew that she had to be firm. On the pretence that she had brought new recipes with her from England, she taught him how to cook several dishes on the modern appliances in the kitchen — appliances which, she became more certain as time ensued, he had never before encountered, let alone used. She had hoped Cook would be grateful to her for giving him both the opportunity and the instruction to allow him to learn new skills, but, although he always fawned smilingly to her face, behind her back he showed his resentment, complaining bitterly to his wife and the other servants. Although Elizabeth was aware of this, she forced herself to shrug off her misgivings. Instead she noticed only the way that Cook had improved, which was most noticeable in the food he supplied for the table. She praised him, hoping that he would change his attitude.

While Cook was something of an enigma, the houseboy she had chosen was proving to be a huge success. Cissy, the man whose badly scarred face had so perturbed Melanie, had admitted to Elizabeth that he often drank too much palm wine, but he had sworn on his mother's life that if she employed him he would not touch another drop. Indeed, he would be the most reliable of houseboys. Elizabeth had reservations on this point. She thought it unlikely that he would be able to stay sober long, but in the end she had decided to give him the benefit of the doubt. There was something about him that appealed to her — an eagerness to learn and a need to be valued.

In her eyes, his disfigurement called for compassion and understanding rather than the fear and rejection with which he seemed to be treated. She felt she understood him, and that perhaps it was in her gift to make a difference — maybe even change the course of the young man's life.

The Lion Mountains

Although he had received no formal training in what was required of a houseboy, Elizabeth had been proved right. Cissy learned quickly and easily; he was reliable; he had indeed given up the drink; he smiled more — a somewhat fearful grimace, but an indication of happiness. He began to do tasks even before Elizabeth asked, such was his devotion to her.

- 6 -

THOMAS FREE, MAKE-HOUSE MAN

Elizabeth was keen to trace the young man who had rescued her daughter from the jungle and then simply melted away.

"Who was the young man who brought Melanie back?" she asked Cissy.

Cissy looked to the ground and shrugged. Actually, it was Thomas, his cousin, who had picked Melanie up and carried her for some distance. No white man or woman would countenance their child being carried like that, he thought. Thomas was in very bad trouble. No wonder he had disappeared.

"Surely you know, Cissy? I'm sure he was the man behind you in the queue."

Still Cissy refused to look at her. He shrugged again and Elizabeth saw a tremor shake his shoulders. His face, so far as she could see, was scowling, making his ugliness more pronounced.

"Cissy!" she cried, losing patience with him. "I'm sure you know who he is! You *must* tell me. I insist."

Cissy shifted from one foot to the other, head down. All at once, everything became clear to Elizabeth.

"You think I wish to punish him!"

The note of astonishment in her voice caused Cissy to raise his eyes. A brief glance, but sufficient confirmation

The Lion Mountains

for Elizabeth.

"No, no!" she went on hurriedly, "You have entirely the wrong idea, Cissy. I want to *thank* him for finding Melanie and bringing her back. Why, we might never have found her if it hadn't been for that young man! She might have died in the jungle." She shuddered.

Cissy risked a direct glance at her and instantly realised that she had had no intention of setting a trap for him, as he had feared. Noticing the sheen of tears in Elizabeth's eyes, he decided to take a risk.

"His name is Thomas," he offered.

"Thomas! So you *do* know him!"

Cissy kept his eyes lowered but his voice was firmer.

"Yes, mam. Dat boy is cousin of mine."

"Cousin?"

"Yes, him come from same place as me."

Elizabeth smiled. Good. She would drag as much information from Cissy as possible. "What do you know of him?"

"Him good garden-boy!"

"Anything else? How old is he?"

"Thomas strong. Him tall. He say he twenty-one years old."

"Twenty-one? I don't believe that, Cissy! If he were, he would have been called up into the army by now. No able-bodied young man is exempted. I know."

Cissy hung his head again and would not meet her eyes.

"Maybe him younger than he say."

Elizabeth snorted. "Quite a bit younger I suspect."

She hesitated for a moment and then made a decision.

"Cissy, I want you to bring Thomas here to me. Tell him he is not in any trouble. Tell him I only want to thank him. I will put him to the test and, if he is good enough, I will employ him as our garden-boy."

Cissy's ugly face was transformed by the smile that lit up his face. If you looked at his right profile, Elizabeth thought, he was a handsome young man. She determined to find out how he had come by the terrible scar that disfigured him. But that could wait. Right now, she needed to find Thomas before he joined the others and trekked back to his village.

"Go and find him, please, Cissy. And go now!"

"Yes, mam."

Reluctantly, she returned to making the list of all the changes needed in the household. Where to start? Perhaps with Thomas? Yes, they needed a garden-boy and Thomas deserved something for rescuing Melanie.

The newly appointed houseboy ran from the room, but it was another half-hour before a breathless Cissy returned, accompanied by a tall good looking young man whom Elizabeth recognised.

"This, Thomas," Cissy said by way of introduction, pushing the young man forward, so hard and unexpectedly that Thomas' long bare big toe brushed against Elizabeth's shoe. He quickly snatched his foot away and nearly overbalanced.

Seen close-up, Thomas was an ungainly youth. Tall, with a fresh innocence about him, he was clearly not completely in control of his long limbs. Perhaps he was growing too quickly, Elizabeth thought, and placed his age at no more than fourteen. But that was a good age for a garden-boy. He was young and strong and probably had his mother and several younger siblings to support.

"Him good boy," Cissy was continuing. "Thomas, he have many, many sisters and his father gone away longtime. His mother say he need job very bad."

"How do you do, Thomas?" Elizabeth asked automatically, her mind a whirl of possibilities.

"How do you do, madam?" Thomas replied, his English enunciation perfect. Elizabeth was surprised into an amused smile. No doubt some missionary had taught him that simple but effective phrase, she thought, and laughed.

The laugh shocked Thomas. His eyes opened wide, exposing the whites around his startled deep brown irises.

Elizabeth was quick to make amends: "I'm sorry, Thomas. I'm very well, thank you. Now, I would like to thank you for finding my little girl and bringing her back to me."

She held out her right hand and, at a nod from Cissy, Thomas took it gingerly, as if he wasn't sure what to do with it. Elizabeth gave his hand a brisk shake and released it.

"I understand that you were hoping to apply for the post of garden-boy?"

Thomas nodded.

"Well, then," she continued, "The post is yours. Shall I discuss the details with Cissy?"

The boy looked at Cissy, who responded by giving him a quick dig in the ribs. "Yes, please, mam," Thomas gasped. "Please, I go now?"

"If you wish," Elizabeth said formally, suppressing a smile. "Perhaps you would like to go and tell your mother? But I shall need you here at eight o'clock sharp in the morning. You understand?"

"Yes, mam … yes, mam," Thomas mumbled as he backed towards the door. "Eight o'clock sharp, mam. Tank you … tank you very much, mam."

Appointing Thomas was one thing, Elizabeth thought. Finding a way to use him in a garden that was barely more than a quarry site, was quite another. She caught herself up on the ungenerous thought, remembering how, almost before she had put a foot in the door, Harold had insisted on taking her round the garden: admiring the view, demonstrating where he thought a sitting area would be most pleasant, purring with delight over the terraces he had had constructed and showing her with pride the few blades of grass that were the beginnings of a lawn. 'How Englishmen love their lawns!' she thought, smiling. Such a vain idea — planting a lawn to make such a foreign land look like 'home'. The climate was impossible for 'proper' gardening, so Mrs Carey had informed her, being so wet in the rainy season that everything sprouted, and far too dry in the hot season for anything short-rooted to survive.

But Harold had taken her arm and delightedly revealed the present he had acquired for her.

"I know you won't believe it, but I managed to find *this* in the market."

If he had been a magician producing something completely unexpected from out of thin air, Elizabeth

The Lion Mountains

could not have been more surprised by what was revealed when he drew back a tarpaulin roughly draped over a long box, shorter than a coffin but of much the same dimensions.

"A croquet set!" he'd crowed, opening the box with a flourish and producing four croquet mallets. "All complete and in perfect condition — most surprising in this country where usually *nothing* is complete because someone 'borrows' part of it for a purpose entirely disconnected from its original use. But here we have four of everything."

Glancing into the box, Elizabeth saw instantly that the central marker post was missing, but she said nothing in the face of Harold's pleasure, preferring to thank her husband profusely for his gift. She smiled both at his boyish enthusiasm and over his attempt to plant a croquet lawn especially for her. Without bending to inspect it, she could see that the grass seed with which it was sown produced a rough coarse covering that bore very little resemblance to the silky croquet lawns of England. 'He has tried so hard to achieve something special for me', Elizabeth thought. Touched by his tenderness, she felt her heart fill with love for him.

What to do with Thomas?

The question circled round and round in Elizabeth's mind. Harold liked to direct all that happened in the garden, which was his joy, relaxation and pride. Thomas would no doubt soon learn to mow the lawn and weed the beds, but at present his knowledge of the cultivation of foreign plants was zero and the lawn was too young and sparse to be mown.

What to do with Thomas?

A project was needed. Something interesting, but simple enough for Thomas to manage on his own. Elizabeth racked her brains but could not think of anything. She asked Cissy.

"Him very good with goats, mam," he told her.

"But we have no goats!"

"Plenty goats in market, mam," Cissy responded. "Cook, he say dey dam good goats in market. Very good milk, he say — and very good eating, he say too."

"And I suppose he would like to keep a goat or two in the servants' compound? So that they could supply fresh milk for my morning tea, I suppose?" she asked with a sarcasm that was lost on Cissy, whose face broke into a grin.

"Yes, mam. Is very good idea, mam. Cook, he be most pleased, mam! Goat milk very good in tea. Dem goats be no trouble, no trouble at all!"

Contrite, Elizabeth tried again.

"I'm sorry, Cissy. I have confused you because I did not make myself clear. No goats. Master doesn't like goats. Goats eat everything. Goats go everywhere. Goats are not good. *Definitely* not good."

"Mam, dat cook, he like goats very much," Cissy remonstrated. "Him no like Cissy, him no like Thomas, but him like goats very much."

"I know, Cissy," she softened and then relented. "I'll ask Master tonight when he returns whether we can buy a couple of goats. But I was asking about Thomas … what else can he do?"

"Him good mend-house man, mam."

The Lion Mountains

"Mend-house man? Do you mean someone who does repairs to houses? A carpenter? A builder?"

Cissy was looking confused.

"Mend-house man? Explain to me, Cissy."

"If hole in roof and water come in, Thomas, he mend-a da roof. If chicken flying in window, Thomas he put wire in da window to stop him chicken dead!"

"Ah! So he helps to mend the village houses?"

"Yes, mam!" Cissy nodded enthusiastically.

"So ..." Elizabeth spoke slowly, turning over the idea in her mind before she put it into words. "Do you think Thomas could build a little house for Melanie? Like a small village house for her to play in?"

"Oh, no, mam!" Elizabeth blinked in surprise, but Cissy was still speaking: "Thomas him very good make-house man. Him make very good, very big *white man's* house for Missy!" And Cissy's wide white smile was a joy to behold.

The white woman hid her desire to laugh, realising that it would be misunderstood. To Cissy's chagrin, she explained that she wanted Thomas to build a very small African village house for Melanie. Cissy reluctantly agreed to tell Thomas, but his disappointment that Thomas was not to build a proper white man's house was abundantly clear.

Elizabeth, however, was delighted. It seemed she had hit upon the perfect compromise — a project to keep Thomas busy and a special treat for Melanie who loved playing mothers and fathers with her dolls and was always asking for her own Wendy House. This would be much better — her own authentic African villager's hut, something for her to boast about when she returned to England and something that would always remind her of Sierra Leone. Perfect!

The next morning, Thomas presented himself to Elizabeth promptly at eight o'clock, wearing well-worn but newly washed and pressed shorts and a grey T-shirt to which he had pinned something at heart level. Intrigued, Elizabeth asked if he would let her see what it was and Thomas carefully unpinned his decoration. In the palm of her hand he placed a piece of paper on which he had drawn a flower — a very elaborate flower — each petal coloured in with crayons and carefully cut out. It was a beautifully crafted thing and she told him so as she handed it back to him. But how strange that he would prefer to take so much trouble drawing and colouring a paper flower when there were the most magnificent natural ones to be found in the jungle.

"Him flower no fade," he said. And Elizabeth realised that Thomas knew what she was thinking. If she wanted to keep her thoughts to herself she must be careful to guard them well, and her facial expressions, too.

"It's beautiful," she said and meant it, appreciating the skill and time that he had put into its making. She waited while he re-pinned it.

"Now, Thomas, I have a special job for you. Cissy tells me that you are very good at building houses." Thomas gave her a sideways glance, showing the whites of his eyes. "I would like you to build a small play-house for my daughter."

"Missy Melanie," he said, "She small-baby girl: she

no know about jungle. Him very danger-full."

"Quite. That's why I would like you to build her a house in the garden so that she can play safely where I can see her."

"What mean 'build'?"

Elizabeth realised she had flummoxed him by using a word he did not know.

"Make," she said hastily. "I want you to make a house for Melanie."

Thomas' face split in a wide, mischievous grin and he danced a little jig of joy, arms flapping by his side.

"Yes, mam! Thomas Free — him make very good house for mis-mam!"

"Good. That's settled then. Come with me Thomas. I will show you where I would like you to build it."

Elizabeth led the way onto the upper terraced lawn. What a grand name for a small, newly seeded area, she thought, smiling inwardly. She had not discussed a possible site for the house with her husband because he had left for work early that morning, before she was properly awake. But she knew that Melanie was the apple of his eye and, since the house was for her, Elizabeth was certain he wouldn't object.

"Here." The sweep of her hand encompassed a vague area of turf. The black boy eyed the place, his anxiety clear to see.

"But boss, him say this boy must no walk on him lawn until him grass grow very big," he said guardedly. "Cissy him done tell me. If any boy walk here, boss man be very angry."

"Don't worry, Thomas, it is all right. I will talk to my

husband and explain. He will not be angry with you, I promise."

Thomas would not meet her eyes: hanging his head he said: "No mam. Thomas he very sorry, but he no can make-house here if boss he no give permission."

Elizabeth took a deep breath and then let it out very slowly, allowing her annoyance to dissipate and with it her anger. There was no point in being angry with Thomas. She should have realised that here in Africa the status of a woman, even a white woman with authority, not only depended on the status of her husband but was also inferior to it. If Harold had said the lawn was not to be walked upon, the lawn would not be walked upon. She sighed. It would certainly not be walked upon merely because the boss's wife wanted something done. But she knew very well that should it be necessary to take a short cut between houses, or to pick a few ripe red chillies from the many chilli bushes that had miraculously presented themselves all over the garden, or to chase the chickens back into the compound, then Harold's orders would simply be forgotten, or, she preferred to suspect, be judiciously ignored.

Noticing the flash of startled concern from Thomas' eyes, she appreciated the courage of his refusal. But to back down would jeopardise her authority over the servants. All she could do was to change tack.

"Oh dear, no. Of course you can't start making the house yet, Thomas. You need things to build it with. Cissy will...."

"No need, mam!" Thomas was grinning again. "Thomas, he go in jungle, find sticks and ...and ..." He tried to indicate what he would collect from the jungle by miming it so extravagantly that Elizabeth laughed.

"Very good, Thomas. You go and gather what you need. Tomorrow my husband will give you instructions."

As Elizabeth had surmised, Harold, while not pleased at the possible desecration of even a small part of his beloved and much-watched-over lawn, had resigned himself to it as soon as Elizabeth had told him of her surprise for Melanie.

"All right, Old Girl, I suppose so," he reluctantly agreed. "But don't keep it as a surprise — Thomas will take a while to build a house, however small it may be. And it will be good for Melanie to take part in its construction, or at least to see how it's done."

Elizabeth accompanied him outside where Thomas was waiting, absently scraping his toes in the bare soil of the nearest flowerbed. Harold frowned.

Seeing this, perceptive Thomas hurriedly smoothed the earth back into place with one foot as he was surveyed from beneath bushy grey brows. The youngster flushed under the scrutiny.

"You'll do. You've been a garden-boy before?"

"No, boss." Thomas informed him cheerfully. "But Thomas Free, he very good make-house man."

"You look very young to me. Are you sure you can do this?"

Thomas nodded. "Sure, boss. Very strong." He demonstrated his strength by bunching the biceps on both arms.

"I believe you. Do as mam says and get this house built wherever she tells you. You understand?"

Thomas nodded again.

"Good. No nonsense though! I want this house built without delay."

"Yessir, boss!" The garden-boy saluted.

"Good. Now get to work, my boy."

Elizabeth accompanied her husband as he ambled up the drive to where the company car was parked, with Maurice waiting patiently at the wheel.

"Thank you, darling. Think how happy Melanie will be."

"You make us both happy," her husband mumbled, kissing her ear before he disappeared into the dark recess of the vehicle.

"Melanie!" Elizabeth called, clapping her hands.

Hearing her mother's summons, the little girl appeared as if by magic, her doll cradled in her arms. Elizabeth held out her hand to her daughter.

"Right-o, darling. Let's decide on the best place for this house."

Melanie felt shy. She knew that it had been Thomas who had carried her out of the jungle. She recognised the shininess of his black skin, the strong swaying movement of his thin waist above the loose waistband of his shorts, and, most of all, the unique warm smell of him — a sort of musky, musty, salty odour.

Now, with her hand firmly tucked into her mother's and with Thomas walking two steps behind them, she was very aware of his presence. She didn't know why she was shy of him, but maybe it had something to do with the feeling that she was at home here in Africa as she had never felt at home before — except in England, of course, because that was her very own country with her very own relatives, her brother and aunts and uncles and cousins and grandparents, and dogs and pigs and cattle and sheep and hops and the odd cat or two that slept outside in the barn and caught rats and mice for their supper, occasionally bringing in a trophy and laying it at her mother's feet. She heaved a great sigh. Yes, England was special, but there the weather was cold, while here in Africa it was hot, warming her right through to her bones.

In Africa no-one wore many clothes, unless they were European, like Mummy and Daddy, or Creole, like the 'top brass' in Freetown. Melanie wasn't quite sure what 'top brass' meant but she thought it had something to do with being important, and of course important people had to wear clothes to show they were important. It was so clear to her: if no-one wore clothes, then they would all look alike and it would be impossible to tell if anyone was more important than anybody else.

In Africa it was more comfortable to wear fewer clothes than in England, which she thought was very sensible. She herself wore only a sleeveless short sundress and sandals — and a pair of knickers underneath, of course, so you couldn't see her bottom if she bent over. Perhaps that was why the black women wore long skirts, she thought — so they didn't show their bottoms. But they didn't mind showing their bosoms. The bosoms were fascinating in the way they moved, and because they were all different shapes and sizes and even colours — and the nipples were all different shapes and colours too. Some were dark jet black and some almost purple while Cook's wife's nipples were a sort of dark pink like the inside of her lips. And yet, Melanie mused, African men didn't stare at the women's bosoms the way European men did: nor did they try to look down Mummy's neckline like Colonel Parry and Mr Watson did.

Melanie revelled in the hot liberating African sun. You didn't have to wear so many clothes, so if you touched someone it was likely you would touch warm skin and not cold cloth. And the sun made people happy. You could see it in their smiles and in the wavy way they walked with straight backs and swaying limbs: gracefully, free. Because they carried everything, even huge heavy big things, on their heads, they did not seem so weighed down by their burdens and the corners of their mouths went up instead of down. All the little children had bigger sisters and brothers to look after them, and there was often a toddler or baby for them to look after as well. She sighed. She would have loved a baby sister, or even a brother. Although perhaps she wouldn't want a baby brother so much because she already had an older one of those, her beloved Trevor.

African children were allowed to play outside all day without having to wear a hat to prevent them getting sunburned. They stamped and splashed in the muddy puddles after the rain. They plunged into the sea and swam underwater. African children paddled under the waterfalls in the creeks and took their showers there. Some of the older boys dived right down to the bottom of the deep, deep pool where the washing was done by their mothers, coming up so suddenly and so close that they would startle the women into dropping the black soap they used, so the boys would have to dive down again to retrieve it. And when they surfaced their mothers would be laughing-cross, and would swipe at them with a wet cloth or playfully box their ears.

African children wandered along jungle paths to find firewood or to forage for odd jungle fruit that *her* mother said were inedible — which meant they would give you tummy ache if you ate them: but only if you weren't African, because Africans ate peculiar things like the funny shaped groundnuts in their paper-like wrapping. Mummy said you had to know how to prepare groundnuts properly — which meant to cook them for hours — or else you could die from tummy-gip.

"Melanie! Did you hear what I said, darling?"

Melanie started, drawn back from her daydream by her mother's tone.

"Thomas is going to build you a house here. Won't that be lovely?"

Melanie's face lit up with joy. She had always wanted a house of her own so that she could play mummies and daddies properly.

"A house for me, Mummy? Oh thank you!" she breathed, hardly able to believe her good fortune.

"And ..." her mother began.

"And thank *you*, Thomas!" Melanie said, taking her mother's 'and' as a prompt to good manners.

Thomas' face broke into his wonderful ingenuous grin and Elizabeth smiled.

"I was going to say that Thomas is going to show you how he does it! Won't that be fun?"

Melanie looked from her mother's sweet patrician face to Thomas' wide, beaming features.

"Oh, yes! It will," she said.

To Melanie, the house took a long time to complete. Not long before she had accompanied her mother on the journey to Sierra Leone, her friend Carol became the proud possessor of a 'Wendy House' which her uncle had sent all the way from America for Carol's eighth birthday. Melanie had coveted this modern miracle from the moment she first saw it. She didn't mind at all that it was made of plastic. It reminded her a bit of the old military tent that her uncle sometimes erected in the garden in summertime so that the three of them, herself and her cousins, Anne and Jane, could sleep outside under the big elm tree. All the girls knew sleeping outside was a huge adventure. She and Anne loved sleeping in the tent and would chatter late into the night until they fell asleep, but Jane was annoying because she would start to sob when the dusk began to fall and they would have to take her indoors to her mother. Still, she was only a little girl then, Melanie thought judiciously, three years younger than me and Anne.

The tent was fun but shabby: Carol's Wendy House was superb. Boasting a red roof, it was shaped like a real house, square rather than tent shaped, and on the outside the walls were made to look like real house walls, white, with pretend plants — all green squiggly stems and bright yellow flowers — growing up them. Above the painted plants were windows that looked almost like real ones. It was a pity they didn't open but they did have clear plastic in the middle that you could see through.

The Lion Mountains

The door was a disappointment, though — just a flap of material that looked a little like a door, but was really a kind of curtain. Still, the Wendy House was special. Not *one* of her other friends had anything similar.

She hoped her house would be made of proper house materials like bricks and tiles, with a real fire and a chimney and perhaps even a kitchen in which she could cook wonderful meals for Bluebell and her sisters before she put them to bed in their cots.

She asked her mother about it.

"Oh no, darling! This will be much more exciting than a Wendy House — and very different from an ordinary house. You will have a very special, *extra-*ordinary house! Thomas is going to build it specially for you."

They chose the spot where Melanie wanted it to be, close to the edge of the higher lawn terrace: so that it would drain well, her mother said, and under the big cotton tree with the swing so it would not get too hot inside and would be sheltered from the heaviest rain. Straightaway, Thomas fetched a big stick and Melanie drew an outline on the grass. Thomas and her mother considered for a bit and then Mummy said she thought it would need to be a bit bigger and Thomas said he only knew how to build round houses. So they considered a bit more and while they were doing that Melanie clambered onto the swing because Bluebell wanted a go on it and she would keep falling off unless she sat on Melanie's lap.

In the end, her mother drew the outline of the house and told Thomas to make it like a round house but with straight walls and if he had any difficulty the boss would tell him what to do.

Although, to Melanie, the building of her house seemed to take forever, in fact it was constructed very quickly. In the early morning, Thomas would go into the jungle and find what he needed. As the sun began to rise further into the sky, he would work assiduously, his long limbs and back almost steaming in the heat. When the thunderclouds rolled across the sky at noon, he would return to the compound to eat with Cissy. Like the sun itself, he would reappear when the rain lessened and work solidly for an hour until the heat grew unbearable, even for a native. Then he would find a place to sleep for an hour or so — occasionally in the shade under the car, sometimes in the garage, but most often in the cool beneath the swing tree.

Occasionally, Melanie would find him there when she came down from her own afternoon rest, hoping that the house would be finished and ready for her to use. If she found that Thomas was asleep she would tiptoe up to where he lay on a simple woven mat. Often he would wake immediately, no matter how quietly she approached, but once she was able to gaze down at his sleeping features. His skin was so smooth and black, his face so reposed, his eyelashes so long and curly and his lips so full and pouting that he seemed like one of the strange creatures she had heard about when Daddy read 'Gulliver's Travels' to her. To Melanie he exuded a simple fascination — he was so familiar and yet so different from all the other people she had ever met.

She knew a little about different cultures because her

The Lion Mountains

mother and father had taken her with them on their travels. Thus, she was aware that different races peopled the planet. So far, having become accustomed to Arabs of various nationalities; learned that although German and French people looked like Englishmen and women they spoke a different language and ate very different things; and that Pakistanis and Indians were of similar skin-colour and proportions, ate similar food (mostly curry) wore brightly coloured clothes and chirruped the same sort of language. Her father said the thing that really distinguished one nation from another was religion. For instance, the Indians were mostly Hindus and the Pakistanis mostly Muslims. Melanie thought that was a very difficult distinction. How could you be sure what nationality they each were? You couldn't see someone's religion from the outside: it was what they thought in their minds and felt in their hearts. And how could you know that by looking at someone?

She could see that Africans were different again: they had a different mentality, her father said, and a happy-go-lucky attitude to life. Although Melanie wasn't quite sure what that meant, it seemed to her that they lived in the present moment: for if it rained they took cover; if the weather was hot they slept; if they needed food, they cooked — or at least the women did; if the boss asked them to, they worked, but not very hard and only if it was not too wet or too hot. 'Tomorrow,' they would say, flashing a smile, 'We will work tomorrow'. They had the same attitude to belongings. Much was shared, but Africans did not appear to mind at all if things were old or shabby or did not match: they treasured brightly coloured objects of all kinds. They took great pride in all their possessions and found unusual ways of using them. Melanie remembered seeing a toothless old man riding on a mule. He had been seated in a tatty old armchair with its legs roughly sawn off that had been roughly tied in place with a piece of sacking. On his head he wore a woman's old straw hat and he waved a banana leaf fan to keep the flies away. He had managed to keep his dignity despite the odd form of transport.

She had gazed down at Thomas until the young man, becoming aware of her scrutiny, had leapt to his feet and returned to his task with barely a fleeting smile in her direction.

The house rose from the earth as if it were an exotic jungle plant.

First, Thomas pushed in stakes he had cut from the jungle. He measured their distance one from another by eye, leaving a gap of approximately a foot-length between them. Then he took more pliable sticks and wove them between the stakes, alternating the weave to give the walls stability. When the walls were completed, he bent the uprights over so that they joined in a ridge which he strengthened with another pole. Onto the roof structure, fortified with more canes, he fastened overlapping palm leaves to form a thatched roof. To make sure it was both rain and wind proof, Thomas battened down the palm fronds with yet more canes. Unlike most village houses, Melanie's house had windows that opened. Her father had suggested this and enjoyed teaching Thomas the technique of making window frames. The windows were unglazed, because glass was unnecessary in that hot climate: a through draught kept the interior both cool and dry.

Melanie was delighted with the house. When it was finished, Melanie invited Thomas to tea and they sat on the floor and ate pretend sandwiches and drank pretend cups of tea.

And the next day Melanie rounded the corner of the house to a wonderful surprise. Thomas had made a garden around it: he had dug two flower beds either side of a short path. The path was paved with pale, whitish pebbles and he had edged the flower beds with white stones: in them he had planted pink wild flowers, knowing pink was her favourite colour. All around the house he had dug a trench to take the rain water away and he had continued the trench right across the rest of the lawn to where he knew the water would soak away. Melanie caught her breath, equally delighted with the garden, and fearful of her father's response to the disfigurement of his precious lawn.

But when Thomas wandered around from the other side of the house, trying hard to appear aimless and unconcerned — although unable to hide a grin as broad as her house was wide — she so far forgot herself as to hug him hard in thanks. She determined that she would say that she had asked Thomas to make the garden and dig the trench. That way she hoped to save him from her father's wrath.

The next day, when Melanie came down to breakfast another surprise awaited her, for there, carefully propped up against her juice glass, was a small piece of paper, completely covered in fantastical drawings and carefully coloured with crayons. Melanie looked on the front and on the back but there was no clue as to the artist or who had placed it there.

Her mother asked Cissy if he knew.

"Thomas Free, him think Missy would like."

"Ah, Thomas," Her mother half-sighed through a gentle smile. "Of course! I should have guessed."

"I do like," said Melanie, politely. She put the piece of paper in her pocket, and so began a collection of Thomas' drawings. On each of the next three mornings she found another offering.

On the fourth morning, her mother suggested that she should draw something for Thomas. Rather against her will, Melanie drew a picture of her house. She turned the drawing over and frowned.

"How do you spell Thomas?" she asked her mother. She wrote: *'To Thomas, thank you for making my house, from Melanie'* on the back, before folding it up and giving it to Cissy to deliver to Thomas.

Melanie spent many happy hours playing in her house. She was used to being a solitary child and enjoyed having a special place of her own. Often she would see Thomas and they would share a smile but the easy relationship that had connected them when he was building her house seemed to fade. Now he had other jobs to do round the garden and Cissy had informed him that it was not appropriate behaviour for the garden-boy to talk to the master's daughter as if she were one of his little sisters.

Her mother too frowned slightly on her becoming friends with Thomas. After all, he was employed as the garden-boy: he was a servant. Also, he was learning more important things. Cissy was teaching Thomas the skills required of a houseboy and he had a lot to learn. Elizabeth tried to explain to her daughter that Thomas' prospects were very different from hers. He was a poor village boy whose father had gone into the hills to search for diamonds — a dangerous occupation because the mountains were filled with brigands — and it was likely he would never come back. His brothers were in the army and had wives and children of their own, so it had fallen to Thomas to provide for his mother and younger sisters and the best way he could do that was by working for Europeans and learning new skills. Gently, she told Melanie that she and Daddy were doing all they could to help him but it was difficult because he was illiterate.

"What's illiterate?" she asked and her mother said it was when people had never had a chance to learn how to read and write, so they couldn't do either of those things. Melanie thought that was amazing. Why, it was the first thing she had ever learned! And so long ago that she couldn't even remember a time when she didn't know her letters. She loved reading. What would it be like not to be able to read a book? Her mother had always read her a bed-time story, making it a special time of closeness between them. Melanie still loved to be read to, but she loved to be able to read quietly by herself even more.

"Didn't his mother read him bedtime stories?" she asked. She remembered her big brother reading to her by the fire in the sitting room. Didn't Thomas read to his sisters like Trevor did to her?

"No, darling. You see, there are no books in the

village and his mother cannot read or write either. But she has taught him lots of practical things like how to build a house."

Melanie nodded, but she was astonished. It was wonderful that he could build a whole house from things he found in the jungle, she thought, but what a pity that he couldn't read and write.

Melanie had always loved teaching her dolls. Often she would set up her blackboard on its easel and write big letters on it in white chalk so that they could learn how to write by copying what she had written there onto the small blackboards she had placed on their laps. She made little paper reading books for them, too. Bluebell was very lazy and always waited for Melanie to help her but Teddy and her other dolls were much better pupils. Thomas was often to be seen peering in at the window and sometimes Melanie would see his lips moving as she taught her dolls how to read.

Melanie wondered whether Thomas would like to learn his lessons too, but she was too shy to ask and anyway he was far too old. Mummy might say he was only a boy but she knew he was a man.

Then she had a brilliant idea. She would teach him to write by writing him notes.

- 7 -
AFRICAN HEARTBEAT

The drums started that night. Melanie had just fallen asleep when a deep pounding rhythm penetrated her dreams, a constant dum-dum-pause-dum-dum that reverberated through her whole body and set her bones shaking.

The rhythm interweaved with her consciousness: becoming ... no, *being* part of her ... her own heartbeat, her divine essence ... strangely relaxing as if she were lying against her mother's breast feeling the pumping rhythm of her heart against her cheek ... aware of the vital connection between her mother's heart and her own, the primal beat, the over-lighting energy of Life that existed before all matter was shaken into form.

Melanie felt this deep in her core, even though she had no thoughts, no words, no knowing — only an unconscious inner understanding of the pulsating beat that vibrated through her, running down her spine before fanning out to embrace her head, her arms, her hands, her chest. It resonated in her abdomen and reverberated down each limb, until her feet could not keep still, as if returning the rhythm to the echoing earth.

For one long moment, knowledge and understanding merged into the silent vastness of a universal and hidden truth. She perceived the secret of the Universe: but only for a moment. She shivered — and the secret was forgotten, lost amongst those smaller truths that littered her efforts to comprehend.

The primal beat of the bongo was but an echo of the earth's ancient rhythm. Her heart beat out the same tattoo: dum-*dum* pause dum-*dum* as, with dreams for wings, she found herself aloft, flying towards a village somewhere deep in the African jungle.

A ring of huts formed the perimeter of a circle around which the beat travelled, relentlessly building into a crescendo of sound. For within the perimeter, another ring had formed: dancers gyrated round a centrepiece of three carved stools on which reposed the tribal chieftain and his two most trusted advisors, in their hands the staffs of office that designated their rank and office.

Around them dancers sang and swayed and pranced and leapt in time to the rhythmic thump of the drums: drums beating out the vital soul of Africa, the rhythm of a thousand feet, echoing through a thousand years. Now, a deep voice sang out above the others, calling them to respond: forty voices answered him, upraised in unison, pounding out the rhythm of the words, dancing their meaning into action.

The rhythm changed. In an instant she was there: a dancer amongst the dancers, black as they, powerful as they, her long grass skirts tickling and slapping at her bare lower legs, bead necklaces a-dangle round her neck, breasts naked, proud and firm: swaying, dancing, stamping in time with the beat, feeling the vibration deep within her body, hearing the ancient sounds issuing forth from her throat. She was one with the circle, one with the

The Lion Mountains

tribe, and one with the land on which she stood.

As the beat continued unassuaged, the dancers too, entranced by the pulsing tempo, shook their shoulders, their arms, their hands, their hips, their ankles, their feet: gave themselves up to the temptation of Eve, to their innate knowledge and reverence for the Earth.

The tempo changed and quickened, became more alive, enflaming, angry. The unforgiving rhythm beat through the drumming hands faster and faster: as faster and fiercer, the dancers sprang and jumped and twisted and turned. Mouths opened, eyes started, chests heaved and still the unrelenting drummers drummed: drummed until their palms were bruised and sore: dancers cavorted until their feet could pound no more. Only then did the drumbeat slow, and slow some more − until a solitary drum beat out a slow death and the dancers tumbled to the ground. Breathless, their chests heaving, they lay full length upon the Earth's skin and allowed her sweet coolness to invade their glistening limbs.

And the moon rose. Round, yellow and full, she poured the balm of her silent presence upon the fevered place below, where dark form after dark form rose softly from the earth and melted into the shadows. Melted away − until only the chief remained, regally upright, still and stiff upon his stool of state. Then he, too, rose to his feet. Saluting the moon's silent majesty, he bowed with naked dignity before striding out of the moonlight and into the darkness of the jungle.

And, as the jungle drums slowed and died away outside, Melanie slipped into deep, dreamless sleep.

* * *

In the morning Cissy was no-where to be seen.

The sound of electric machinery had woken Elizabeth. She checked her watch. Cissy must be up very early this morning, she thought. But when she came down the stairs, she found Thomas in the dining room.

"Good mornin', mam." He beamed at her, carefully wheeling the electric polishing machine over the floor boards and then across her precious wool carpet.

She looked around, words failing her. The table had been laid, but there was no smell of fresh bread wafting through the dining room: and why was Thomas …? Before she could ask, Thomas turned the machine around and it began to roar its way back across her precious floor covering.

She put a hand to her mouth and mutely surveyed the damage. Luckily the garden-boy had just begun this chore, making only a few passes with the machine. But the carpet bore the brown marks of its twisting brushes.

"What are you *doing*, Thomas?" she shrieked, the words out of her mouth before she realised.

The young man's face fell. He stopped pushing the machine and shouted back over the din.

"I is doing chores for Cissy."

"Where *is* Cissy?" Elizabeth looked around as if expecting him to materialise from thin air. In response to her impatient gesture, Thomas switched off the machine.

"Cissy, him bad, mam."

She frowned. "Bad? What do you mean?"

"Him very sick, him no can get up from bed, mam."

"Why not?"

Thomas shrugged. He stared at his bare toes, the

picture of discomfort, and would not meet her eyes. "Him very sick," he muttered.

Understanding dawned. Cissy had asked for permission to go to the jamboree down in Freetown. No doubt he had drunk too much and was now suffering from a hangover. Inwardly she wanted to laugh, but she knew that she must not show her amusement if she was to keep discipline.

Cissy chose that moment to reel through the door from the servants' quarters, clutching his head. His eyes were shut and he staggered into the dining table, balanced himself against it and, with obvious reluctance and enormous effort, slowly opened one eye. Closing it swiftly, he doubled over.

"Cissy!" The sharpness in Elizabeth's voice brought him to attention.

"Sorry, mam, Cissy him no feeling good." The houseboy tried to straighten his back but the movement brought on an attack of retching and, one hand to his mouth, the other to his forehead, he rushed from the room.

Gathering her wits, Elizabeth turned to Thomas. "Thank you, Thomas. I think that's enough polishing for today."

"But, mam, Cissy him say Thomas must do polishing. Him say houseboys know how polish. Him say…"

"Yes, Thomas, I'm sure you'll make a very good houseboy in time. But that is not the way to use the polisher. I will make sure that Cissy teaches you when he is better."

Thomas bowed to the inevitable and was about to

wheel the polisher away when Elizabeth asked curiously: "Were you with Cissy last night?"

"Yes, mam."

"Where did you go?"

"We go Freetown, mam. To big-time dance. Cissy him drink lots, him very happy!"

"I can see that," Elizabeth commented, dryly. "So what time did you get back?"

"When him sun come up. Cissy him very happy."

"Goodness! How did you get back? You must have walked?" It was a long walk, six miles or so and up-hill all the way. Elizabeth felt she had to admire the effort they must have made so that they could be at work on time in the morning.

"No, mam! Cissy he danc-a all de way!"

- 8 -

SHIVERS

After the 'night of the drums' as Melanie called it, strange things began to happen: well, perhaps not strange, but odd and peculiar things that made her feel a little wobbly inside as if the world was not quite safe. Melanie found herself thinking this and told herself she was being silly. Of course the world was safe! Her world was safe, anyway, because she had her mother and father both together, which wasn't always the case. They all lived in a lovely house and had a car with Maurice the driver who always smiled properly as though he meant it, like Thomas did. And there was Cissy to do all that Mummy wanted round the house and Cook and his wife. But perhaps that was the problem, she thought, there was something about Cook, something she didn't like, something that made her shiver, and yet he always grinned at her. And if he had one eye that always seemed to be looking over your shoulder when the other was looking directly at you — well, that was his misfortune, as Mummy said, something he could not help.

But just thinking of Cook's one wandering eye made Melanie shudder. Cook looked like a toad, and even though she rather liked toads and the funny croaking sound they made, you wouldn't want to touch one, would you? They looked ugly and slimy and just a little bit evil, like the Devil in the pictures that illustrated her Bible. The Devil was black with horns on his head and a leer that made him look wicked. He was always hiding somewhere where you could hardly see him, waiting to trick you or trip you or hit you over the head, especially if you were a disciple, or even Jesus. One of the pictures showed Jesus praying on a mountain and the Devil was at his shoulder whispering in his ear, trying to make him do something like throw himself off the mountain and survive — which might have meant that Jesus would not have been crucified and then there wouldn't be any Christians which was a horrible thought. But quite a good idea in a way. How wonderful it would be to float down a mountainside and not hurt yourself and not be crucified either.

Melanie opened her Bible and found the picture she remembered. The Devil looked murderous — he was tempting Jesus, saying one thing with honeyed words while wanting to push him off the mountainside. Then she saw the likeness. She closed the Bible abruptly and hid her head in her hands. Cook had that same expression in his good eye when he looked at her mother. She suddenly felt cold as she realised that Cook was wicked. She must tell her mother, but how? And when?

Before she realised about Cook, there had been The Spider. Melanie always thought about it with a capital S because it was so huge. One night she had woken suddenly with a jolt, not knowing what had woken her and shocked by the suddenness of it. She opened her eyes and lay very still in her bed. She could hear her heart thumping. Above her on the wall was the biggest

Spider she had ever seen. Its furry brown body was the size of a large mouse. Motionless it balanced on crooked legs like double-length pipe-cleaners. But it was its red shiny eyes that most frightened Melanie. Scared that The Spider might drop on her, she slowly slid under the sheet. Slowly, slowly she slithered down the bed and out at its foot. As her head came free of the covers, she risked a glance towards the Spider. Although it had not moved, she was certain its eyes were following her. With a gasp, she raced silently for the door and into her parents' room. She crept in beside her mother and shook her awake, more with the trembling of her body than her shaking hands, whispering in her ear for fear the Spider would hear.

Elizabeth had been dreaming that she was running through golden wheat fields wet from the early morning dew, while, so high above as to be invisible against the deep blue summer sky, a skylark was singing his hymn of joy to the world. Reluctant to exchange her dream for an awakening in the steamy heat of an African night, she nonetheless awoke instantly, swept the bed sheet aside, and swung her feet to the floor.

"Where is this monster Spider?"

"In my bedroom, I think. Unless it followed me?" Melanie was still shaking.

"Come with me." Elizabeth held out her hand to her daughter, feeling the clammy small one slide into it. "Good girl, now bring the chamber pot. Got it? Good."

Softly they stole from the room onto the landing. And stopped short. The Spider stood squarely in the centre of the landing floor as if challenging them. Its eyes glowed fiery red in the moonlight. 'Good God,' thought Elizabeth, 'It's the size of a dinner plate.'

"Go back to Daddy," she whispered. Melanie retreated ... but only as far as the doorway. Elizabeth picked up the chamber pot and cautiously crept forward. She was within an arm's length of the Spider when it leapt at her. Raising the chamber pot in defence, she dropped it in fright, and looked around frantically, wondering where the Spider had landed. Melanie was pointing a shaking finger. Elizabeth swallowed a nervous snort of laughter. The chamber pot had landed upside down and from beneath it protruded two hairy legs. A 'bonging' sound was issuing from it as the Spider tried to free itself.

"What is it?"

Harold emerged from the bedroom, in his hand the big flit-gun which he was brandishing like a weapon.

"Just a Spider," Elizabeth said with a spurt of the laughter. "*Only* a Spider."

"All this fuss over a spider," her husband retorted sleepily. "Here, give it a blast of this. I'm going back to bed."

Elizabeth used the gun to spray insecticide all round the pot. Then she waited. The spider's legs retracted slowly and the bonging stopped. Carefully she eased the flit-gun's nozzle under the pot and sprayed again. Retracting it just as carefully, she placed the gun by the pot and tiptoed back into the bedroom. Melanie flung her arms round her mother's neck and soon all three of the family were cuddled together in bed. Not for long because it was too hot, and, still sleeping, they moved apart. Soon the morning light crept over the window sill.

Awake, and seeing her husband and daughter still fast asleep, Elizabeth crept out onto the landing to investigate. No Spider's legs were sticking out from under the chamber pot. She raised the container a little. No movement. Deciding to throw the Spider out, she crept back into the bedroom and picked up the pad of paper she kept for writing letters. There were only a few sheets of paper left so she tore them off the pad and slipped the cardboard backing under the pot. Carefully she lifted the whole caboodle, but at that precise moment Melanie came out of the bedroom and bumped into her. The cardboard slipped and the Spider fell at their feet. Dead. They looked at it in disbelief.

"It's dead," said Melanie.

"Yes," her mother agreed.

"Is it the same Spider?"

"It must be."

"But it can't be! It's too small."

Elizabeth checked the inside of the pot.

"It's the only one that was under the pot."

Melanie poked at the dead arachnid with her toe. It was certainly a very large spider and its legs were curled up under it, but she still wasn't convinced it was the same one she'd fled from in the night.

"But it's not the *huge* Spider that was there last night!"

"I know." Elizabeth was as puzzled as her daughter. The spider she'd trapped had been the hugest she'd seen in all her days abroad, and yet the one at their feet looked about a quarter of the size it had been the night before.

"It must have shrunk as it died."

Harold, of course, thought it was a great joke that both his womenfolk could have been so scared by a spider. It was certainly a large spider, but not the monster that Melanie insisted it had been. But Melanie and her mother knew better: when alive, it had been a monster Spider. Of that they were both convinced.

After that, Melanie and her mother checked her bedroom for Spiders every night and made sure that the fly screen across her window was properly secured. After a while it had become a game, played with much laughter.

A few nights later, soon after Melanie had been snuggled down in bed, the drums started again. The rhythm was slower and more persistent, but the drums were few and the drumming did not last long.

The next night, and the next, the drums spoke. Each night they spoke for longer, became more insistent and were joined by others. The following night they were silent. Melanie lay awake waiting for the thrumming beat to begin, but all she could hear were the usual night sounds: a birdcall, the hum of a mosquito or two, a slight breeze rustling the leaves. Eventually she slept.

A sunbeam was playing across her eyelids. She muttered and turned over. Into blackness. For a moment she was puzzled, then, suddenly she was fully awake. The room was in darkness but a bright beam of light was darting around the room. It came from the direction of the window. What could it be? It reminded her of the time Mr Watson had walked her and her mother home.

The Lion Mountains

Why? Mr Watson had shown the way with a torch. A torch! That's what the light was.

She quickly shut her eyes, squeezing them tight. What should she do? Perhaps she should just lie still? But it might be a burglar! A burglar? Ooh, that was really frightening. She risked a quick peep: apart from the thin beam of light, which was steadier now, all she could see was blackness. She concentrated on the place the light was coming from, screwing up her eyes to focus. Slowly her blindness faded. She could make out the edge of the window and behind the source of the light was a rounder shape. It was a head. As her eyes focussed, she made out the whitish shape of a rictus grin and the glimmer of a reflection on the whites of dark *human* eyes.

Someone must have climbed up to her window with a torch held in his teeth. For now an arm was flailing through the window … breaking *through* the fly screen. Through a gaping hole in the white cotton netting a hand was waving something shiny and metal like a blade.

A shr-rumping sound. Scissors! Someone was cutting with huge long-bladed scissors, like the ones her mother used for cutting material when she was dressmaking.

Suddenly what little nerve she had left deserted Melanie. Her feet hit the floor hard. With a sobbing cry she fled from the room.

Elizabeth was awake before she was even aware that she'd heard Melanie's cry, her response instinctive. She reached her bedroom door a split second before her daughter threw herself into her arms. The child was hysterical, tears falling like rain.

"What is it, darling?" Elizabeth forced herself to be

calm although her heart was racing in fearful bafflement. Her daughter had never behaved like this before.

Melanie sobbed even harder, words bubbled from her lips but made no sense. Elizabeth held her at arms' length and said quietly. "A bad dream?"

Elizabeth felt Harold hurtle past the two of them, heading into the child's bedroom.

"Hey! You! What the bloody hell …!"

Melanie froze and stopped crying with a hiccough. In the sudden silence, mother and daughter, heard a scraping, a thump, a cry of pain — and the man of the house swearing like a trooper.

"The bastards!" Harold stalked back along the landing and raced down the stairs. Elizabeth hugged Melanie to her, reassuring her that Daddy would deal with everything, but the child continued to tremble. Shock and fear, thought Elizabeth.

"Come darling, let's have some tea."

She poured a cup for each of them from the Thermos flask on her bedside table. Elizabeth found that a cup of tea was soothing when she was unable to sleep, or, on the rare occasions that she slept all through the night, a familiar comfort when she awoke. They could hear Harold thundering about downstairs and the rattle of a key in the lock as he opened the front door and peered outside into the darkness of the light.

"I've checked every room," he told them on his return, embracing them both. "So far I can find nothing missing. I looked outside too, but all I could see were a couple of figures racing away across the lawn."

"What did they want?" Melanie asked, no longer

trembling now that her father was close. She felt safe next to his bulk. "Were they *burglars*?"

"Very likely," he agreed, "But if so, they didn't take anything. I think our little burglar alarm here scared the living daylights out of them — whoever they were."

He sat down beside Melanie on the bed and accepted a cup of tea.

The following morning Elizabeth discovered that thieves had indeed been at work. In Melanie's bedroom, one of the curtains at the window hung by no more than six inches of material, the thief's handiwork obvious in the sunlight. So the mystery was solved: he had been after the curtains, which were made of beautiful material she had brought out to Sierra Leone from England. Unobtainable here, she supposed the material would have been worth a good deal in the market.

Elizabeth found herself sighing with relief, but she was still puzzled. She had checked all the other windows. Not one of the curtains had been harmed. She spoke to her neighbours. None of them had found anything amiss. No other curtains had been slashed. Nothing had been taken.

Now Elizabeth began to be really concerned: it seemed they alone had been targeted. Or to be correct, it seemed that Melanie's room had been selected. But why? And what for? There were more expensive curtains at the more accessible downstairs windows. Why climb up to the first floor where a child would be frightened? In the main, Africans were kind and considerate to children.

The more she considered, the more perturbed she became. Something, someone, appeared to want to frighten Melanie. Or worse, to do her some harm. Why?

Elizabeth decided to ponder over this for a while, but she had a feeling she already knew the answer. If only she could work out what it was.

Meanwhile, the drums again found their voice. Now their beat was slow, ominous and chilling. Elizabeth heard in them all the menace of Africa, the deep, thrumming, threatening, primal power that emanated from the deepest recesses of the continent.

Africa's rocks sang of her power; her soil glowed red with power; her tumbling rivers raced with it; her murmuring jungles throbbed with it and her mountain fastnesses thronged with it. The deep throated drums roared with her power; birdsong thrilled with her intensity. Africa's powerful energy, crashing in the ocean rollers, hammered her beaches, battering the rocks of her seashores. Mountain and valley, river and sea, town and village, all reeked with the primeval smell of her might. Violence, anger, disease, poverty all walked with it. Aliveness accompanied it; death followed it. Deep in her heart, Elizabeth recognised it, Melanie was born with it, Harold had suffered for it. The great pulsating heartbeat of Africa encompassed the whole of the human spirit, uplifted and dashed it and ultimately took it back unto herself. And the drums continued to beat out Africa's rhythm … pulse with her rhythm … pound out her rhythm.

Melanie too, heard the drums speak, but to her their speech was familiar, speaking to a deep strong love that she only half-remembered. A dream of warm molten darkness encompassing all possibilities, where a continuous beat signalled life and nourishment. A deep cavern roofed with glittering stars, every one a promise, a potentiality.

The drums' rhythm reminded her of the sound of her mother's heart when she laid her head against her bosom and her mother stroked her hair. Or the warm pulse that twitched in her father's jaw when he was thinking. Or the flapping of a bird's wings. Or the steady drip, drip, drip of water from the eaves after heavy rain.

On the third night the sound changed. A small change: very small: minute. But a sinister change. A change that spoke of death rather than of life; of evil rather than good; a change that Melanie recognised, ice shards in her veins, shivering in the warmth of a tropical night.

Towards dawn, the drums stopped.

"How did you sleep, darling?" Elizabeth asked, holding her morning cup of tea out of harm's way as she held up the bed sheet invitingly. A sleepy Melanie was standing in the doorway to her parents' room, rubbing her eyes. "Come here and let's have cuddle."

"What was that noise last night, Mummy?" Melanie asked as she climbed into her mother's bed and wrapped her arms around her.

"Ah! Did you hear the drums? I thought they began after you'd gone to sleep."

Melanie frowned. "But what did they mean, Mummy?"

Elizabeth paused before she replied. How could she give her daughter an answer when she did not know herself? Harold had explained on her arrival that, on special occasions and celebrations, distant drumming might be heard from the Mende village a couple of miles away, but the kind of drumming during the previous night had been completely unexpected.

Harold himself had been perturbed by the sounds in the night, Elizabeth knew, and she wondered whether he too had heard something menacing in their rhythm, something deep and violent. She felt a tremor run through her body, but said lightly:

"I don't know, darling. I think we shall have to ask Cissy or Thomas. But first, you can share my breakfast here, if you like."

Eating breakfast together was so ordinary that by the time they had finished every crumb of toast and every finger-lick of marmalade both mother and daughter had forgotten the unease that the drums had engendered in them.

Not so, Harold. While his wife and daughter were sharing their breakfast he was on his way to work, his heart still beating too fast and unevenly for comfort. He had never before heard drums played so long, or in a way that induced fear in his heart. He almost imagined there was a message within the sound of the drums: they seemed to foretell danger, for in their constant repetition there was something menacing, something almost demonic.

He caught his thoughts before they spun away into the panic he could not admit: panic that was the legacy of his time in the Second World War and which he had so far managed to conceal from Elizabeth. He had not told his wife that when he had questioned Cissy early that morning, the houseboy had looked at him sideways, showing the whites of his eyes in a bewildered, terrified manner. When pressed, Cissy had muttered something incomprehensible, and, refusing to look directly at Harold, had run from the room.

Harold gave himself a mental shake, lit another cigarette from the stub of the one between his fingers and breathed the smoke deeply into his lungs. No time now to wonder about a possible message in drums, he decided, I have a job to do. And a difficult job at that. I need all my faculties about me and all my courage. No doubt it was something the natives were up to, some ceremony with which he was unfamiliar. Nothing more.

When he stepped from the car, smiling and confident, not one of his employees suspected the anxiety still churning in his stomach.

Elizabeth had noticed that Cissy was not himself. She wondered whether he had indulged too much in the bottle again, and smiled ruefully to herself. She was prepared to overlook his weakness this time, she decided, provided he carried out his duties properly. But whether or not Cissy had drunk too much, she knew his odd behaviour had something to do with the drums that had spoken deep into the night.

Melanie was asleep some nights later, when an odd sound invaded her dreams. She had been dancing on a stage, the prima ballerina in Swan Lake. She was in the middle of a pirouette when she felt a jolt and heard the tearing of material. She looked down to discover that her tutu was being peeled away. A large dog had found its way onto the stage, seized the tulle of her costume and, as the unconcerned stage hands stood and watched, it ran out through the stage door and along the street, pulling the material. Faster and faster her tutu unwound and she found herself spinning with it, pirouetting round and round on one toe, whirling like a dervish. There seemed to be no end to the whirl, no end to the material as she became more dizzy by the second.

The ripping, tearing sound grew louder. Another sound, like the padding of soft feet and the rasping of breath purposefully breathed. With a slight tug of resistance, the last of the tutu's stitches parted and she saw the tulle float past. The whirling stopped and she collapsed to the stage floor, panting. A sea of faces was staring down at her, so close that their breath was hot on her face. Hot, with the stench of rotten meat.

Where was she? A heartbeat later, she recognised the familiar soft mattress beneath her. Now she perceived the comforting walls of her bedroom around her. But she felt herself panting and her heart was beating unusually fast, her prone body instinctively reacting to impending danger. Something alive, something dangerous, something that even now was looming over her. Feeling the weight of it all around her, she dared not move, hardly dared to breathe. Holding her breath, she raised her eyelids enough to peer through her lashes — and quickly closed them.

Was she still dreaming? She knew she wasn't. What

she had seen was real. Now, what to do? Keep still? Feign sleep? Slowly she opened her eyes fully, hardly daring to breathe.

A huge wildcat was watching her, its unflinching yellow eyes boring into hers. Transfixed, she froze, wide-eyed in amazement. The wildcat was nearly as big as she. In the half-light she made out orange stripes in its smooth dark fur. Her heart flipped as she remembered the ginger cat called Marmalade who loved to sit close to the kitchen range at home in England. But this cat was five times the size of Marmalade.

The wildcat's jaws parted, revealing a rough curled tongue. Melanie watched in fascinated horror as it hissed through its teeth; its foetid breath revolted her, but she dared not look away. The animal dropped lower. She felt its increased weight as, on either side of her body, its legs pinioned her to the bed, holding her captive.

Yellow eyes held her mesmerised, yet she knew she must not withdraw her gaze. Into her mind flew the image of her eyes staring into Marmalade's: the cat was always the first to look away. That was what she had to do now. She had to outstare the wildcat and assert her will over the animal. She must pretend to be unafraid and try to work out what to do next. But what *could* she do? She felt her anger rising.

"Melanie!" Her mother's form, a darker part of the darkness, standing in the doorway.

The wildcat's head turned towards Elizabeth, but Melanie could feel it crouching still lower, so close that she felt the quickening rhythm of its heart.

"Are you all right, darling? I thought I heard a funny

noise."

The cat made a sound halfway between a snarl and a mew.

"What's that, darling?"

Melanie realised that her mother had mistaken the noise for a sob and the hump of the cat's body for her own. She was coming closer, moving quickly. Melanie felt the cat shift, readying itself to spring.

Without thinking, she hurled the sheet back over the feline, and herself with it. Together child and beast crashed to the floor, Melanie landing on the wildcat's flailing body, the cat viciously fighting against the restriction of the sheet wound round its body, the child striving to free herself from the animal's violent struggles. A tangle of limbs, a flurry of movement, a cry and the wildcat was free.

The animal launched itself past Elizabeth onto the landing where it stopped, turned and, flicking its tail, hissed through its bared teeth. For a long moment it stood still, lips drawn back. Spitting. Glaring Malevolent. Mother and child were held immobile in that yellow-eyed glare until, realising that the creature was both cornered and terrified, Elizabeth drew back a step, drawing Melanie with her.

Sudden but silent, the cat crouched and then leaped towards them, flashing past so close that its fur brushed against Elizabeth's arm. In one leap it cleared the bed and flew out through the open window.

Open window? The window was open! Elizabeth gasped. Had she not earlier carefully closed it all but a crack and made sure that the mended mosquito net was

The Lion Mountains

safely drawn across it? Each night she checked the window and had made especially certain to do so since the incidents of the Spider and of the thieves.

"Mummy, you closed the window. I know you did!"

Melanie was looking at her in astonishment. Elizabeth slammed the window closed and locked the catch.

"We'll investigate in the morning, darling," she promised, gathering the child to her. "Let's try and sleep a little more, now. Do you want to come in with me and Daddy?"

Melanie was late down to breakfast next morning. Although she had decided to stay in her own bed, the incident with the wildcat had kept her awake, alternatively hiding beneath the bedclothes and clasping the bed sheet under her chin, eyes open wide as she listened. What if the wildcat had come back and brought its mate? What if they liked eating little girls? Her mother had said the cat was frightened and that was why it had hissed and spat at her, but Melanie thought that it had looked fierce rather than frightened.

Melanie was so sleepy that she was still clasping Bluebell under one arm. Normally the doll would have been left upstairs because Melanie had decided that she was too old to take Bluebell everywhere. But today Melanie didn't want to leave Bluebell alone in the bedroom in case the wildcat came back. Wildcats might have a taste for dolls.

She was still pondering these things when her mother appeared, pausing to take a deep appreciative breath.

"Good morning, darling! Don't those rolls smell

delicious?" She dropped a kiss on the top of Melanie's head as she passed her. "What a good bread-maker Cissy has become!"

She seated herself in her usual chair at the end of the table which gave her a wonderful view of the garden through the French windows. As though he had been waiting for his cue in the wings of a theatre, Cissy entered.

"G'mornin' mam. You all right, mam? Cissy he hear you done have a visitor in the night. Some very big, very monster cat he done creep in up da stairs. Is true, mam?"

Elizabeth smiled: a knowing, resigned smile. The way that information travelled around the compound never ceased to amaze her. No servant had been on the premises when the wildcat had made its entrance and she, or rather Melanie, had dealt with the intruder in no uncertain fashion. How then, had Cissy come to hear of the incident?

"I'm fine, thank you, Cissy. Yes, it's true, but no-one was hurt and I think the poor animal was much more frightened of us than we were of him. How did you hear of this?"

Cissy lips twitched as he essayed a smile.

"Cissy, he done have dream." He looked away and Melanie saw that the smile had become a scowl. "He done dream of dat one — very big cat," he added. "And he done dream bad things happen to mam and missy."

"No, Cissy. It was nothing. Don't worry about it. It was only a cat."

Much to the surprise of both Elizabeth and Melanie, Cissy threw himself on his knees in front of Elizabeth,

The Lion Mountains

tears streaking down his cheeks.

"Mam, you bin very good to Cissy. You trust Cissy. You show Cissy how to make bread. You save Cissy. Him bad man before. Him good man now."

Startled, Elizabeth began: "Cissy, you have more than repaid all my trust in you ..."

"No, mam, you no understand! Cissy, him bad man. Him drink too much. Him very, very bad." He hiccoughed, and his shoulders heaved in the effort to contain his sobs.

"Cissy, I am beginning to think that perhaps you drank a little too much palm wine last night!"

"No, no, mam," the houseboy interrupted. "Cissy he swear, he no drink las' night. He no drink at all."

Elizabeth softened.

"I know, you don't drink often now, Cissy." She touched the top of his grizzled head, and at her touch, Cissy looked up. "You always watch out for me. I really appreciate it. But nothing happened. There is no harm done. No need to distress yourself so. Really. No need."

"Cissy done see things, mam. And Cissy done see something las' night ..."

Melanie saw her mother glance at her before flashing a quick warning frown towards Cissy.

"I think you should tell me about that later, Cissy. After breakfast, when Missy is outside playing in the house that Thomas Free made. Then we will have our usual meeting and I will give you my orders."

Cissy's eyes had followed Elizabeth's. He understood her message. Rising to his feet as gracefully as he had gracelessly thrown himself down, he inclined his head.

His lopsided half smile stretched his mouth. "Very good, mam."

"And Cissy — this is very good bread. You have become an excellent baker. Thank you."

The houseboy's smile widened.

"Cook him say Cissy's bread no good. He done say it need palm oil in it."

Elizabeth shuddered. "No, no! Do not listen to him, Cissy!"

"Mam and missy like eggs now? Dem chickens lay very good eggs."

"Yes, please, Cissy. Lightly boiled, like I showed you."

Elizabeth smiled at her daughter, but Melanie couldn't help but notice the shadow of concern in her mother's eyes as she watched Cissy leave the room.

Elizabeth had tried to earn Cook's respect by treating him with fairness and consideration. In all her previous dealings with servants, this strategy had served her well. But not so with Cook.

She simply did not understand the man. Why did she engender in him such enmity? Like her daughter, she was well aware that he hated her. It was more than disdain, more than disrespect. Unused to such behaviour, she had endeavoured to earn his respect and loyalty. She had been firm, but fair. She had tried to reach him, to make him understand that all she required from him was good work and civility. Indeed, on several occasions she had tried to make her peace with him, to guide him so that he could keep his employment.

Regretfully, she had to admit that she had failed. She

saw now that her actions had, if anything, made matters worse. Cook had interpreted her consideration as weakness, her orders as insults. Any attempt she made now to improve the situation would only serve to inflame his sense of self-importance, for he had not an iota of self-discipline and esteemed no-one but himself. Politeness and deference were unknown to him. Certainly, he could not hold his liquor, becoming more violent with each mouthful of alcohol he drank. She suspected that he was bordering on insanity.

Elizabeth decided to take Cissy into her confidence, and found, to her surprise, that the houseboy was in total agreement with her assessment of Cook. Utterly relieved, he confided in his employer all that he knew. He divulged that Cook's wife clearly feared for her life and that his children feared and avoided him. When he was in a rage, whether drink-induced or pure uncontrolled anger, they disappeared into the jungle, often not returning for days. Unfortunately, because of his brutal nature, Cook was treated with complete deference in his home and this had made him expect everyone to obey him. Cissy also revealed that every member in his tribe was aware of his malevolent, violent nature and trod gently around him, fearing his ferocious and unruly temper.

Cissy's confirmation of her assessment worried Elizabeth more than she liked to admit. There had been something peculiar about recent events. She ran over them in her mind: the spider, the thieves, and worst of all, the wildcat. She had made light of all these happenings, but her concern had grown further with each occurrence.

Although she knew it to be completely irrational, she feared that Cook had put a curse on her, and in order to achieve maximum damage, he planned to apply that curse through Melanie, the person closest to her heart.

She was not sure how to put this to Cissy, or indeed, whether she should. She was apprehensive that she would put him in a situation of divided loyalty, or worse, that he might leave her employ. She need not have worried, for Cissy was keen to unburden himself. He had endeavoured to convey as much when he spoke to her at breakfast. His relief now was so great that he beamed, his ugly face cracking into a beautiful smile.

It turned out that Cook had not only made life difficult for his employer, but for all the servants, including Maurice. He had demanded their obedience to his whims and fantasies of importance, using blackmail — he would inform boss that they had committed crimes of which they were innocent — and use threats of violence to coerce them. They had submitted by giving him cringing service, and handing him a proportion of their pay.

But when Cissy had discovered that Cook had visited a witchdoctor and paid for a curse to be put on Elizabeth, the houseboy had become alarmed. He had heard of the Spider and was certain that it had something to do with Cook. Sure enough, he had found a witch-doctor's fetish in Melanie's bedroom. He destroyed it, but said nothing, hoping that its destruction would be sufficient to lift the curse.

Then one evening, he had seen Cook prowling round the house after dark and, fearing for Melanie's safety, had

The Lion Mountains

decided to keep an eye on him. Cissy enrolled Thomas' help, but Cook had almost outwitted them, for, after seeing Cook safely sleeping in the compound, Thomas had dozed off and so had almost missed discovering the intruder who was climbing into the child's bedroom. Melanie's scream had woken him suddenly. He had grabbed the man by the leg just as Harold appeared at the window above, and had narrowly missed being knocked down by the thief's falling body. It had not been a complete disaster, though, for Thomas and Cissy had chased the man off the premises. Harold had seen three figures running away. But, luckily for them, darkness had covered their identity. They had caught the man on the edge of a jungle path and, cajoled with threats of bodily harm, he had confessed that Cook had blackmailed him into attempting the robbery.

Cissy was now keen to bring the man before Elizabeth, but she preferred to wait because she wanted an opportunity to discuss all she had learned with her husband before taking any action that might alarm Cook into further wickedness.

"What do you know about the wildcat?" she asked.

Cissy hung his head. He had stopped watching, he said, thinking Cook would stop when he realised that his crimes were known. Later, however, he had heard rumours about the wildcat: how a trapper had found its lair and killed its kittens for their fur; how, when the cat had attacked him in defence of her pitiful young, he had netted it and taken it back to his village, where he had kept the animal unfed and tethered in the darkness of a hut; how he had encouraged children to poke it with sticks to make it vicious, as he reckoned there was money to be made from arranging a wild animal fight.

But before the trapper had found a fighting opponent for the wildcat, Cook had learned of the animal and managed to buy it for an amount of money far in excess of its value. Cook himself had climbed the ladder, opened the window to Melanie's room and let the famished, tormented cat out of its basket prison.

Cissy had not witnessed any of this, but Cook's wife had been hiding close by, behind a tree. Seizing the chance to have her husband apprehended, she had whispered the truth to Cissy early that morning, asking him to inform the mistress.

On hearing this, Elizabeth decided to act immediately. Thomas was dispatched to Freetown with a note for the Chief of Police, and before the end of the morning Cook had not only been sacked, but arrested. Harold applauded Elizabeth's prompt action, for within an hour of his arrest the whole atmosphere of both the Russell's household and the settlement had changed. An impromptu party followed with much music and dancing and sufficient palm wine to give Cissy another headache.

Once the bully was in custody, many people came forward and many were the charges laid against him. In due course it became clear that it was likely he would be imprisoned for a considerable time.

Once Cook's scowling presence was gone, Elizabeth taught Cissy the rudiments of cooking and before long he had far out-classed Cook in his culinary arts.

The drumming that had so discomfited her

quietened, became more rhythmic and joyful, and gradually ceased altogether. Although she knew it most unlikely, Elizabeth could not rid herself of the idea that the drums' frightening intensity had been a warning to her of intended harm towards her daughter. No matter now, for at last she could breathe freely and allow herself the luxury of relaxation and enjoyment. The whole atmosphere around the house had changed and finally it felt like a home. Her husband and daughter were cherished and happy. And all the while, Africa continued to weave her spell of lush beauty, rhythm and smiling faces around them all.

All too soon it would be time for Melanie to return to England, but until that time came, Elizabeth intended to make sure that they enjoyed every minute of every day.

- 9 -
WE IS TWINS

The dining room was empty, but the table had been laid in readiness and the mouthwatering smell of freshly baked bread suffused the room.

Melanie seated Bluebell in the empty chair next to her own, placed her own handkerchief on the doll's knee as a napkin, chose a white roll from the bread plate and commanded her not to make crumbs on the carpets in case they attracted white ants. She was scrambling into her own chair when she noticed that someone had placed a little posy of red hibiscus flowers on her plate.

"Thomas," she thought smiling. Sure enough, beside the posy lay one of Thomas's notes.

The writing lessons were proving fruitful. At first, Melanie had tried to undertake the project secretly as a surprise for her mother, but it was not long before she realised that the results she desired would be attained much more easily and quickly with her mother's help. Elizabeth had been delighted at the prospect and it had turned out that Thomas was an excellent student, although he would always prefer drawing to writing.

Melanie picked up the latest of Thomas' letters to her. Unlike his previous missives, this was a whole foolscap sheet of paper that had been folded into four like a card. On each face there was a fantastical drawing of jungle plants, jungle flowers, and one where jungle beasts were glaring out from between the waving jungle fronds. But it was the figures drawn in the foreground that caught Melanie's attention: two simple, stick-like figures but both easily recognisable, one tall and black and wearing shorts, the other a small white girl in a coloured dress. They were holding hands. She turned the page and read what was written there. 'We is twins'.

Melanie caught her breath as she read the words.

How silly! She thought. *Of course* Thomas and I *aren't* twins! Twins are born at the same time and have the same Mummy and look alike and always wear the same clothes as each other.

"What do you have there, darling?"

Melanie jumped. She had been so deep in her thoughts that she hadn't heard her mother approaching.

"Just a letter from Thomas," she said, showing her.

"Isn't that beautiful, Melanie? It must have taken him such a long time to draw — it's so intricate and so beautifully coloured. We must buy him another box of crayons. He must have sharpened the last ones right down to stumps with all the colouring he's done for you recently."

Melanie looked again at the drawing. Yes, It was pretty. Yes, he could draw much better than she could. But it was so different from how she drew. It was all curves and no empty space anywhere. And why draw flowers and leaves and colour them in with crayons? Especially when no crayons could ever be the same amazing shades of green and blue and scarlet and puce and purple and indigo and crimson as the real jungle.

The jungle was at the very edge of the lawn so she could see it every day. And so could he.

"And did he bring you those flowers, Melanie?"

The little girl nodded. They were very beautiful. She looked out of the window. Flowers were everywhere, blooming in every colour under the sun, from the huge flamboyant magenta blossoms that festooned the jungle vines to the tiny creamy flower-ettes on the chilli bushes.

Outside the house, colour shone and sang with light, flirting with the darkness before banishing it to the depths of the jungle where it stayed until noon. At midday darkness swept out of the jungle and down the mountain until it overtook the light. Daily, thunderclouds menaced the sun into great heaving tears that bounced off the hard surface of the house and drive, flooded the garden grass, chastened the vegetation and turned the roads into streams. Thunder rolled continuously; lightning flickered and flashed in the heavy darkening sky; rain washed the daylight from the day. For twenty long minutes nothing dared venture out. Then, as suddenly as it had begun, the storm would end, the sun would break through in a stream of brilliant light, the shining roads mirroring its dazzling intensity. Steam would rise in a thick white mist that hissed, goose-like, as it dissipated. From the jungle, a warm, thick fragrance would emerge, slinking around the compound like a furtive beast, its potency as dangerous and intoxicating as its ever-hidden secrets.

How could anyone draw that, Melanie wondered? It was impossible. But Thomas had tried.

Elizabeth saw the slight frown between her

daughter's brows and wondered what had occasioned it.

"These are jungle flowers, Melanie. And they are fresh. They only last a few hours. Thomas must have gone a long way into the jungle very early this morning to have gathered them specially for you. You must write a special note to thank him."

Melanie looked at the flowers with increased interest. Thomas must like her although she was not always very nice to him. She knew it was because he seemed so much older than her, and so very different.

She meant to be nice to him, but she was shy, and shyness made her abrupt and sometimes unkind. She was both drawn to him and a little repelled by him. His skin was so dark that it shone in the humidity of the morning. When he was working in the garden she would watch the tears of sweat drip from him, fascinated by the way his muscles rippled beneath his glistening black skin. Then he would see her gazing at him and he would straighten and stretch out his arms and his wide white grin would be directed right into that little bit of her that she thought was hers alone. She would feel her heart beat in a strange fashion. He was so unusual, so odd. Not handsome. How could anyone black be really handsome? But there was something about his smile and his jointed way of walking and his simple goodheartedness that shone out of him and made her want to be his friend. Sometimes it made her want that more than anything. Maybe that was why she was always oddly stiff when she talked to him, or was it the effort of keeping her hands twisted in her skirt?

"Yes," she said, hiding the note under Bluebell's

dress. The note had a Thomas flavour, a Thomas aroma. If she had to write a note to thank Thomas for the flowers, what *would* Mummy suggest she should do to thank him for the Letter? She couldn't shake hands with him. She really, *really* couldn't! Anyway, she wanted to keep the Letter just for herself. She didn't feel ready to talk to Mummy about Thomas thinking they were twins because she knew Mummy would laugh and say it was 'a ridiculous idea'. Melanie wasn't quite sure *exactly* what 'ridiculous' meant but she knew it meant something like 'silly' or 'stupid' — which being twins with Thomas *was, of course*, but something about the idea was making her feel lighter inside.

As soon as she had finished her breakfast, Melanie went in search of Thomas. She found him without difficulty because he was singing as he worked. He was rather aimlessly digging a hole, the muscles in his back bunching and rippling in a wonderful fluid motion. His shining skin wasn't true black, Melanie noticed: it was the deep chestnut brown colour of a well-polished conker, only slightly darker.

Melanie set her little three-legged stool down on the grass in the shade. Her mother said you should never sit directly on the ground because there were all sorts of creepy-crawly things that would bite you. Sitting down, she found herself absent-mindedly sucking her thumb — something in which she liked to think she seldom indulged now that she was eight — while she considered the best way of thanking Thomas for the flowers while informing him that they were definitely not twins.

Thomas stopped digging. Leaning nonchalantly on

his spade, he flashed his white grin at her.

"G'morning mis-mam," he said, using the strange hybrid name he had bestowed on her.

Melanie removed her thumb from her mouth.

"Hello Thomas," she muttered, turning her thumb this way and that, concentrating on the way its wrinkled, spit-covered surface appeared translucent in the sunshine. You could almost see through the skin, she thought, wiping it surreptitiously on her skirt before sitting on her hands to keep them still.

"You done get my letter, Mis-mam?"

"Yes, thank you, Thomas. It was a very good picture."

Thomas threw the spade down and squatted in front of her.

"Yo is my twin, isn't you?" he asked, his grin wide.

"I don't think so, Thomas. How could I be? We're so different."

"But we isn't different, Mis-mam! We is the same."

Melanie frowned. "How can we be the same?"

Thomas paused and pursed his lips together so that she could see the pinkness of the inside of his mouth. It was quite fascinating, she thought, because on the outside — the bit you saw when he spoke and smiled — his lips were so dark, and yet his tongue was quite pink. Thomas was looking straight at her and she felt herself blushing as though she had been caught doing something naughty. She looked away. Thomas giggled.

"See, Mis-mam. We *is* the same: listen!" His long-fingered hands had been hanging limply over his knees but now he held them up in front of him, curled into fists.

"You is *little*: I is *big*." He raised the thumb of his right hand.

"Yes, but …"

Thomas ignored her.

"You is little *girl*: I is big *man*." His index finger sprang upwards.

Melanie opened her mouth.

"But …"

"You is *English*: I, *African*!" Here he sprang to his feet and struck his chest with his left fist. The sudden movement startled her: he could see it in her eyes. He squatted down again, so his eyes were once more level with hers. The middle finger of his right hand opened.

"You fader is *boss man*: my fader is gone away long time into the hills." Thomas' eyes looked a little weepy, Melanie thought. But then he raised his ring finger so that it stood up straight with the others: only his little finger remained in his palm.

She was beginning to see his logic now. Although she didn't know the word 'complementary' she knew it's meaning. Thomas hadn't really meant they were twins: he had seen that they filled each other's gaps so that together they made one glorious mixed-up whole.

"I am *white* and you are *black*! Well not black *exactly*, a sort of chestnutty colour," she chimed in. She grabbed his hand and straightened the last finger, snatching her hand away as soon as she realised what she had done.

Oh! She had actually touched him! And she liked it. His hand was warm and smooth and dry, and the palm was a pale pinkish colour quite similar to her skin when she had been in the sun too long and Mummy said she looked like a lobster. She didn't think it was a good thing to look like a lobster but since she had never seen one, she dismissed the thought.

She sneaked a peep at Thomas and saw that he was smiling the way her brother Trevor did before he gave her a little grudging praise.

"Thomas Free, he *make-house man* …"

"And Melanie Russell, *lives* in the house Thomas made!"

"I is *strong* man, stronger than lion! And you is … you is …"

"I is … I mean, I *am* … weak. Not *very* weak though —because I can carry Bluebell everywhere and not get tired."

"You go in *car*, I *walking!*"

The thumb and two fingers of his left hand were now vertical.

"You live in big white-man *house*. I is living in *hut*. Not so good as one I build for Mis-mam."

"And a very nice house mine is, Thomas, with a lovely garden."

He raised the ring finger of his left hand. Only one finger to go. Melanie giggled. What else could she think of? What else was different?

"I have one brother … do you have any brothers and sisters, Thomas?"

"Me has four brothers in army, plenty sisters — so I is *rich*, you is *poor!*" The young lack man flashed both his opened palms towards her. "But you never mind, Mis-mam, I share all my family wid you! 'Cos *we is twins!*"

Melanie clapped her hands in delight.

"Yes! We are! We're twins!"

And Thomas seized her little hands in his large palms and together they danced a jig all round the hole he had been digging and out onto the lawn where the sun blazed down on their simple pleasure. Melanie threw her arms round Thomas' waist and squeezed hard just as she did with Trevor and her nose was full of the black warm smell of him and she didn't mind one little tiny bit. In fact, it was a fascinating smell and his skin was soft and hot, just like Trevor's after he had been running.

"You're just like my big brother," she said and wished that Trevor was there. But since he wasn't, she was glad that she had Thomas as a sort of brother instead.

"You is my sister," he said and smiled down at her.

Close by, they heard the clash of the fly door.

"Thomas!" Cissy's voice calling. "Thomas Free!" He was looking away from them towards the servants' compound. "Where is dat no good garden-boy?"

Thomas hurriedly unclasped her arms from around his waist and strode back to his task, but she felt the warmth of the grin he flung over his shoulder towards her.

"I is here, Mr Cissy, sir!"

"We is twins," she whispered under her breath, before collecting her stool and heading towards her house — the house Thomas Free had built for her. "Yes, Thomas and me — we is *very definitely* twins."

- 10 -
CONFLICT

One day, her father smiled across the breakfast table at Melanie and asked her whether she would like to see where he worked?

"Yes, please!" said she, and because Daddy was here eating breakfast with her and Mummy and hadn't just hastily downed a cup of black coffee and rushed away, she slipped down from her chair and, without asking, launched herself into his lap.

"Whoa!" he exclaimed, as his coffee slurped against the edge of his cup and a drop or two splashed onto the napkin tucked under his chin. "What's all this about, sweetheart?"

Melanie twined her arms round his neck, bringing her eyes so close to his that her eyelashes flickered against the glass of his spectacles. Hazel eyes looked into hazel eyes and then they both chuckled and she said: "Tickle me, Daddy!" because that was her way of telling him how much she loved him. And he did, because that was his way of telling her how precious she was to him.

Despite gales of laughter and a rumpus that was seldom seen so early in the morning, they were soon, all three of them, stowed away in the huge black car driven by Maurice. Her father was in his usual business gear of long khaki shorts and white short-sleeved shirt, wearing the sandals he called 'chupplies'. Her mother was wearing a simple yellow-flowered dress with a square neckline and Melanie had chosen her favourite blue dress with frills for pretend sleeves.

No sooner were they seated than the car hummed into life and headed up into the mountains. This in itself was unusual, for when Melanie and her mother went out they usually headed down the mountain to Freetown, or to the market, or the beach. Now, Melanie gazed out of the windows as they wove their way along a narrow road, smooth and recently tarmacked, that wound through the mountains. On either side, the land rose steeply. Thick jungle clung to the slopes, except where bare black crags broke free from the vegetation's restraint. As they climbed higher, the rocks grew more numerous and the jungle fell away. After a while Melanie stopped looking out of the window because it all looked the same.

The last part of the journey was very steep. As they drove down a narrow gorge onto a muddy flattened area Melanie feared that the car might flip over and somersault down the hill, but Maurice was a careful driver and well used to the dangerous approach to the engineering works.

Melanie tumbled out of the car as soon as it stopped, feeling slightly queasy. As he helped her mother out of the car, she noticed her father raise her hand to his lips. A tender look passed between them, a still moment in which Melanie felt she was both included and excluded. The moment passed and suddenly the mood altered. A large white man in a bush hat with perspiration beading on his brow and staining both the front and the back of his white shirt, started shouting loudly. All work halted immediately and the man hurried across to where they were standing. Without even stopping to greet them, he took her father's arm and guided him away, talking fast but inaudibly close to her father's ear. She saw him raise his eyebrows in alarm, rub his chin and mutter something under his breath.

"Sorry, Elizabeth, I must deal with this urgently. I shouldn't be long. I'll ask ... ah! Here he is!"

And as her father hurried after the large man, there was Mr Watson, extending his hand to her mother, offering her his arm and asking for the honour of showing her round the site. Her mother accepted both offers, and Melanie ran to take hold of her outstretched hand.

As far as the child was concerned the whole place was very muddy, exceedingly noisy and rather boring. The geologist's cross-section drawing of the mountain's differing rock strata was interesting, and she enjoyed the challenge of trying to interpret the engineering diagrams which charted the progress of the project, but, to her, the whole process of excavating a path for the river through the mountain was noisy and very muddled. Black labourers were running about hither and thither in a way that reminded her of ants when their nest was disturbed.

Elizabeth was far more interested than her daughter. She followed all that Mr Watson told her about placing dynamite charges so that they would have the maximum effect with a minimum of disruption, all of which depended on the length of the fuse and how much rock had to be moved. Already the tunnel had reached two-thirds of the way through the mountain. Now was the time to decide whether to carry on tunnelling from this side of the mountain, or to start excavating from the other side of it, which would require very careful calculation — not that all their calculations weren't careful, he added.

Harold erupted out of his office in the temporary building and marched towards the tunnel. He caught sight of his wife and daughter and stopped suddenly, as if he had temporarily forgotten all about them. Turning on his heel, he hurried to Elizabeth and, drawing her a little away from the others, spoke rapidly into her ear, pointed at the car and kissed her. Catching Melanie up to his shoulder he whispered in her ear, too.

"I'm afraid you must take Mummy home now, sweetheart. I'm going to be very busy for a while and won't have the time to show you any more things today. But I'll be home in time to read you a goodnight story."

And with that he gave her a quick squeeze, set her down on her feet and pushed her gently in her mother's direction. Maurice held the passenger door open for them. Before slipping inside to sit next to her mother, she turned to blow a kiss towards her father, but he was walking fast and purposefully towards the tunnel's entrance and did not look back. By the time the engine coughed into life he had disappeared into its cavernous mouth.

She held her mother's hand tightly all the way back to the house and, in spite of all her mother's efforts to interest her — including playing *what do I spy with my little eye* — Melanie could not forget the look on her father's face. Something inside her stayed tightly wound until her father came home late that evening. Melanie was already tucked up in bed but, true to his promise, he came upstairs to read to her in time-honoured fashion. After he had finished the story, her father tickled her until she had giggled herself breathless. Then he kissed her goodnight, switched off the light and reminded her to say her prayers, which she did — but the knot inside her did not dissolve completely, for his face wore a worried frown whenever he was unaware of her scrutiny and he walked in a funny stiff way that betrayed his anxiety.

Melanie was woken by the sound of her parents arguing, something to which she was not unused. Although their voices were lowered, she heard the worry and distress that underlay their anger.

She tiptoed to the door of their room and put her ear to it.

"I want you to fly home with Melanie," her father was saying. "I have no idea what is going to happen here, but I fear the worst."

"No, Harold, I'm staying. There's no danger now that Cook has gone."

"I fear there is! And I cannot bear the idea that you may be caught up in violence. I would never forgive myself if either of you came to harm because of me."

"I'm staying. And that's an end to it!" Her mother's voice was definite, loud enough for every word to be clearly heard. "I'm your *wife*. We've spent too much time apart already, and you *need* me here. Someone has to look after you!"

"Elizabeth, listen to me! I haven't wanted to worry

you with this, but there are explosives missing from the store at work. A large amount of explosives. Large enough to cause significant damage."

Her mother laughed. To Melanie it sounded forced. "And you think they'll use a large amount of explosives to blow up this house? Is that likely? Surely, if someone uses the explosives to foment civil war, they will target somewhere important, like the barracks?"

"Elizabeth, they have no cognisance of anything beyond their own petty rivalries and a hatred of the British ..."

Her mother interrupted. "No, they need you to finish this project. They know that it will bring prosperity to all who live beyond the mountains. And who else has the fund of knowledge that you possess? It makes no sense to target you — or me, come to that."

"Darling, I must *insist*. You must listen to me. I know what I'm talking about."

"Definitely not! And that's the last I have to say. I'm staying. It will only be for a few months, anyway."

Her mother's voice ended on a shrill note. A pause. Then her father saying something in a low voice, words she could not catch. A muffled noise: perhaps a sob?

Melanie scooted back to bed. Her father — her mother — neither was allowed to cry. The very possibility was incredible. They were her stalwarts, her rocks, the ones who knew everything, who were strong. Maybe it was a cough, she thought. That was it — a cough. Not a sob. Anyway, in the morning everything would be different.

She allowed her eyes to close as her thoughts took her

The Lion Mountains

back to the time when she had asked her father about the reasons for arguments ....

Melanie knew many people thought her father was her grandfather. No-one else she knew had such an old father, though she doubted that he was *really* one hundred and two as he insisted he was every time she asked him his age. But she wouldn't swap him for anyone, even if he did smell of cigarettes and sometimes of whisky. He was the best father in the world.

Mummy sometimes said that Melanie had never known her real father. She said he had lost a part of himself in Burma during the War, especially his easy laughter and infectious chuckle. But Melanie adored her father and he still *did* chuckle when something was funny, even if sometimes there was a strange faraway look in his eyes. There were times, too, when he was subject to loud outbursts of words and his eyes took on a reddish tinge, but such fits of temper were over almost before they began and then his eyes would fill with tears and he would go out into the garden. Melanie would follow him and silently take hold of his belt, waiting and watching as he lit a cigarette with a trembling hand and took a few deep puffs, his eyes raking the sky. Gradually his shaking body would calm and he would look down at her with a sad smile and squeeze her hand.

"Sorry, sweetheart," he would say and she would lead him to the garden seat and snuggle onto his lap. They would sit in silence for a while, and then he would tickle her and she would giggle and they would get up and go back indoors to where her mother would be waiting. Sometimes Mummy would be sad and sometimes she would be struggling to contain her own anger and occasionally she would be smiling.

Melanie would leave them then, before they sent her away. Sometimes she would sit on the stairs and half-listen to their conversation but usually she would go and talk to her dolls and explain that grown-ups were inexplicable. She warned them that they would find that out for themselves when they grew a little older. Why, she herself might even be inexplicable to them! But all they had to do was to wait patiently and quietly and the world would right itself again and everyone would be friends.

Her father had explained that to her, saying that the best of friends fought about things called 'principles' and that, although it was best not to fight, there were times when you had to stand up for freedom and what you think is right. He said that no-one really won in a war, but lots of people were harmed, or wounded, or killed, mostly to no purpose. The best thing about a war was that people found that they were all flesh and blood, no matter which side they were fighting on. Everyone suffered in a war: there were no true winners.

In the end, when everyone was sorry, because everyone was scarred on the outside or scarred on the inside — or, too often, scarred on *both* the inside and the outside — and when both sides had run out of money to pay for weapons, and too many people had been killed and there was nothing to eat because the farmers had been forced to go and fight as soldiers, then, just to survive, everyone would have to agree to live in peace. But, even though everyone wanted peace, often they could not agree on what 'peace' was exactly. And then there were lots of talks and 'negotiations' and eventually there would be a treaty — which meant a long document in which everything that had been agreed was written down — and then there would be peace and everyone would be friends again, for a while.

Her father said that peace was very precious, and that everyone — adults and little girls and countries too — needed to do their very best to settle an argument or a difference of opinion before it escalated into war. Here Melanie would nod sagely and think of the times that she had fought with Anne, who was her very best friend as well as her cousin, and that it was usually over something very silly: something like 'which colour is nicest, pink or red?' When they were very small and disagreed, Melanie would bounce on Anne's tummy, which Anne *hated*, and Anne would twine her fingers in Melanie's hair and pull *hard* — which really, *really* hurt! — and they would *both* be screaming and crying and hurting. And all over nothing — or at least, nothing Melanie could remember now. She wondered whether 'which is nicest, pink or red?' was a principle? Melanie thought that if it was a principle it was a very silly one, and that she and Anne were very silly to quarrel and particularly silly to hurt each other over such a stupid disagreement. She made a mental note to write this down and send a letter to Anne suggesting that they should agree never to squabble again and to live in peace together forever.

Daddy said there were bound to be disagreements and arguments and quarrels but that it was up to her to consider all sides of the quarrel and to act accordingly. She asked what 'act accordingly' meant and he said that it was to do what you believe is right which might well be to apologise, or to accept the other person's apology. He added that sometimes you had to decide to apologise even if you still felt you were right because that was the sensible thing to do, rather than to hurt someone else. But, he added, the most grown-up thing to do was to 'agree to differ'.

Melanie didn't think that was *at all* like grown-ups. They were always fighting — including Mummy and Daddy.

She thought it over and round and up and down, but it still didn't make sense. Eventually she decided to ask her mother about it.

"Mummy, why do you and Daddy fight?" she demanded.

Her mother looked startled. "But darling, your father and I never fight!"

"But you do argue!"

"No, darling, we don't argue either, but we occasionally have disagreements."

"Daddy said it was grown-up to agree to differ."

"That's true, but sometimes you have to differ before you can agree."

This was too complicated for Melanie although she did consider it, her hazel eyes holding her mother's brown ones.

"Yes, but do you agree to differ *afterwards*?" she asked eventually.

"Sometimes. And sometimes we agree with the other

The Lion Mountains

person. But there is one rule that we never break — Daddy and I never go to sleep on our anger."

"What does that mean?"

"It means that, no matter how tired we are, we will always make up a quarrel before we go to sleep."

Melanie widened her eyes. "Do you really?"

"Yes, darling, we do." Her mother laughed and ruffled Melanie's blondish curls. "The first time we quar … disagreed, we both stayed up the whole night. I was waiting for Daddy to apologise and he was waiting for me to say sorry. But we both thought we were in the right, so neither of us was prepared to back down. All night long, Daddy was reading and I was playing patience but neither of us would say sorry. Then the sun came up and we were both exhausted! I looked at Daddy and thought how selfish I had been because he had to go to work all day. And he looked at me and thought of all the things I had to do that day. And we both knew how tired the other was …"

"So — who said sorry?"

"Neither of us. We looked at each other and smiled. And then we hugged and then there was no need to say we were sorry because we weren't disagreeing any more!"

"But how did you know you weren't disagreeing when no-one said sorry?"

Her mother smiled more deeply. "Sometimes — you just know. In fact, we had 'agreed to differ'! You see, darling, it wasn't necessary for one of us to be right: we were each entitled to our own opinion. We recognised that the only important thing was that we loved each other. It didn't matter who was wrong and who was right. Love is stronger than all the opinions and all the words in the world!"

"But you hadn't settled the disagreement, Mummy," Melanie said, frowning. "I don't understand. If no-one said sorry how can you forgive them? How can love be stronger than all the words in the world?"

"We all disagree, occasionally, darling. But the love in our hearts helps us to understand what the other person is feeling."

"And then we love them?"

"And then we remember that anger hurts everyone and …"

"And then we aren't angry anymore?"

"Precisely, my clever little one! And when we aren't angry, we can feel love."

"And then we love them."

Melanie said it as a statement and indeed she was thinking of her disagreements with Anne and how they always felt closer after a quarrel. Until the next occasion. But she didn't want to think about that.

- 11 -

GOODBYE: OCTOBER 1956

As the rainy season settled in, frogs and toads found a haven in Melanie's house, which was not as watertight as Thomas had bragged it would be. But that might be because the rain was so very, very heavy, Melanie thought. She had seen one of the bantam chicks killed instantly by a giant raindrop which fell plumb on its head as it raced for cover. She rescued the little dead body, holding it between her hands and willing life into it as she sheltered in her house, but the warm body slowly cooled and she knew it was dead. She laid it carefully on the table Thomas had made and, as soon as the rain ceased, she went indoors to find a pencil box for a coffin in which to bury it.

That afternoon Thomas dug a grave for the chick and they buried the tiny creature with great ceremony. Thomas had brought a flower which he laid on the tiny patch of dirt and Melanie said the Lords Prayer and they both sang *'All Things Bright and Beautiful',* Melanie's favourite hymn. She had taught Thomas to sing it in the proper way without all the hip shaking and hand clapping and funny breaks at the end of the lines which he affected. She thought it was a very beautiful funeral and that the chick would fly to heaven and into Christ's bosom like all his other children.

A few days after the burial ceremony, Melanie's mother called her.

"Have you been in your house lately, darling?"

"Yes, but I don't like it as much now that there are so many frogs and toads in there," Melanie admitted.

"Perhaps it would be better to play indoors from now on until the rainy season is over," Elizabeth suggested, carefully not admitting that the rainy season would continue now until two or three months after Melanie had flown home to her school in England. "The servants say that snakes will follow the frogs …"

"Why?"

"They like to eat them! And I don't want you to be bitten by a snake."

Melanie didn't want to be bitten by a snake either and so she left the house alone. But she knew it felt deserted and lonely because it looked so sad. She would blow kisses to it out of the window, and even when she was playing in the den she'd made in her bedroom instead, she would pretend she was playing in Thomas-Free-make-house-man's house.

She missed the feeling of the house, of enjoying the fact that it was hers alone and she didn't have to tidy up at all if she didn't want to and was tempted to disobey her mother. One day, the urge to play in the house was so strong that she set out towards it, but a long thin black snake glided across the path in front of her, slithering swiftly in under the door. From that day on she kept well clear.

Not long afterwards, Melanie soon realised that her African days were numbered because her mother started

The Lion Mountains

talking of her flight home and how lovely it would be to see Trevor and Anne and Jane and her aunts and uncles. Elizabeth produced a map and together they plotted the route of her journey. It would take a whole three days and two nights to fly all the way to England, but then it had taken eleven days by ship on the outward-bound journey, so she wasn't surprised.

Her mother enthused about what an adventure it would be. Very few children in the world would ever fly so far on their own. Not that she would be completely on her own, because she would be given into the charge of the stewardess, which meant that she would have a very kind, pretty lady to look after her. The plane would fly during the daylight hours, only coming down to refuel along the way, but in the evening it would land and she would stay in a hotel. Wasn't that exciting?

"Yes," Melanie dutifully agreed, rather doubtful at first. But her mother's enthusiasm swept her away; and when the time came to leave she was excited about the coming adventure. Her excitement carried her onwards on a wave of anticipation which, as her mother had intended, helped to assuage the sadness of leaving Africa.

Melanie found her heart was aching. She loved everything about Sierra Leone, even if it was a bit frightening at times, and the thought of leaving her parents brought tears to her eyes even though she should have been used to goodbyes by now.

"We'll be home with you before you know it!" her father had joked but she knew the months would drag until he and Mummy came back to England. No matter how much she would love to see her cousins and Trevor, and the dogs and Marmalade and sheep and all the other things England offered, she dreaded leaving her house, and the chicks and the servants, even Cissy, and especially Thomas.

Thomas said he would come to England to find her because she was his twin, wasn't she? But first he had to join the army for a while and make some money. And then he thought he would become a sailor on a ship because ships sailed away to exciting lands, even as far away as England. He knew because he had a cousin who was a sailor on a ship that sailed up and down the coast of Africa delivering all sorts of cargo, so no-one in the family ever went short of things.

And while they were talking of this, he would suddenly laugh at her and turn a handstand, or stamp in a puddle, laughing and splashing, and she would join in until they were both wet and weak from giggling. Afterwards he would tease her by saying that there were diamonds to be found in the mountains and all he had to do was to put a pickaxe on his shoulder and march for a week into the jungle to a place where diamonds as big as beans and gold nuggets the size of hen's eggs were to be found in the bed of a secret river. He would dig up the biggest diamond and the largest of the golden nuggets and smuggle them to the gold-buyers who would give him a price so huge that he could buy anything in the world. Even Buckingham Palace and all the guards. So he would be 'Thomas Free - King of England' and he would ask her to be his queen because "We is twins, isn't we?"

Much as she wanted to believe him she knew in her heart that his words held not an iota of truth — they were

The Lion Mountains

just fantasies.

The day of departure came too soon. Her suitcase was packed. Her mother gave her a special little case and helped her fill it with soap and a comb and a flannel and a few sweets and a banana for when she was hungry.

She said her goodbyes as she had been taught, with a smile and a handshake, but Thomas was nowhere to be seen. Cissy said he had gone into the jungle but would be back by nightfall. Melanie smiled. Only she knew that he had gone in search of gold and diamonds.

Elizabeth hated the journey to the airport; hated the prospect of saying goodbye to her daughter and leaving her in the hands of strangers for the flight home; hated even more the prospect of the African house empty of her childish laughter, her quicksilver temperament. She sighed and masked it with a yawn. She had been torn for weeks between her husband and her daughter but in the end she had chosen to stay. Although he tried his best to hide it from her, Harold's need was the greater. Melanie would have much to distract her back in England, but Harold had nothing other than his love for her, a love which brought him many lonely nights as he moved from country to country as project followed project. Each time he found a house where they could live and each time she made it a home. It was the nature of colonial life.

For hours, Melanie had been busily drawing in secret. She clutched the picture in her hot hand as she sat in the car, watching the passing scenery and saying goodbye to each special place and view, but also noticing the conflicting emotions that passed across her mother's face.

Elizabeth dared not weep at this parting. She had told her daughter that the last thing she wanted to see from her was her smile. She must do the same: make this separation easy. And so it was. Elizabeth had ensured they would be late so there would be no prolonged goodbyes. She squatted beside her daughter and hugged her tight.

The stewardess stopped beside them and smiled. "Are you ready, Melanie?" She held out her hand. "You can help me dole out boiled sweets to the other passengers."

"Goodbye for now, darling." Elizabeth kissed the little girl and let her go. "Have a good flight." She managed to smile convincingly, and gave her daughter a gentle push towards the stewardess.

"Goodbye, Mummy. Don't cry. I'm smiling. See!" Melanie smiled first at her mother, and then up at the stewardess whose hand she clasped. And nearly forgot the special thing she carried in her other hand. But not quite. Turning back to her mother, she passed it to her.

"Mummy, please give this to Thomas."

Elizabeth looked down at the crumpled paper in her hand: a hand-coloured drawing of Buckingham Palace copied exactly from the photograph in Melanie's encyclopaedia. On the other side was a picture of Thomas, clearly recognisable by his customary stance and low-slung shorts. Across the top in very curly writing she had written: *Thomas Free - King of England.* And at the bottom: *From your twin, Melanie Russell - Queen.*

When Elizabeth looked up, her daughter and the

stewardess were mounting the boarding stairs up to the plane. When she reached the top, Melanie turned and looked back at her mother. Smiled. Waved.

    Then she was gone.

- 12 -

AFTERWORD

It was a long and tedious journey back to England for Melanie. Although she was delighted to be reunited with Trevor and her cousins, Anne and Jane, and all her other relatives, and very glad to be back on the farm with the animals, she missed her parents and everything about Sierra Leone. Even though she could feel it beating inside her chest, she felt as though she had been ripped away from her heart. Her heart was somewhere hot and humid, where jungle-clad mountains swooped down to wide sandy bays; it beat with the rhythm of the native drums; it danced in the loose-limbed way that African children moved along the jungle paths and it ached when she thought of the way that Thomas smiled at her when he called her his twin.

Her mother wrote to her often, happy chatty letters full of love. Letters that successfully masked the hole that had been left in Elizabeth's life with the departure of her daughter. Letters that were written to cheer Melanie. And so Elizabeth did not tell Melanie that she could not give Thomas her picture because the garden-boy did not return to the household. From Cissy, Elizabeth eventually learned that Thomas had gone in search of his father; into the mountains where diamonds as big as beans were to be discovered and gold nuggets the size of hens' eggs could be found in the banks of a secret river. She gave Melanie's picture to Cissy, who promised to make sure Thomas received it if he ever returned to his village.

Melanie had a feeling that her picture never reached Thomas, partly because her mother didn't mention it or the garden-boy again, and partly because she never again received one of his special missives. But she had kept his 'We is twins' letter and hid it under her pillow when she went to sleep. It was her treasure.

When she grew sad and lonely she would take it out and read it, running her fingers over the beautifully drawn flowers, and her heart would cease to ache as she remembered that they were very definitely twins. Then she would catch the faint Thomas smell from the letter and smile.

When she really wanted to be back in Sierra Leone Melanie would cuddle her furry little lion, wind him up and watch him open his mouth to roar. And then she would remember the days when her mother had said: "Daddy's sending the car back today so we can go to the beach."

"Yippee!" she had cried, rushing off to find her swimming costume and rubber water wings.

Within an hour mother and daughter had found a place to lay out the beach blanket on the sand and, while Elizabeth sunned herself, half-pretending to read a novel, Melanie busied herself building a sand castle.

Looking up from her book, Elizabeth gazed at the beautiful scenery that surrounded them. She sighed with happiness. She was so privileged to be here in this beautiful place enjoying the sunshine and her daughter's company. Privileged and blessed, she thought. So nearly she had been whisked away from her children and husband by the long arm of death; twice she had almost died; and yet here she was, still fragile but still alive, and so appreciative of all that the good Lord provided. Closing her eyes, she breathed a prayer of gratitude. Opening them, the world around seemed clearer, more precise, even more beautiful.

Ahead of her, the sun-kissed Atlantic ocean sent lazy ocean rollers to wash against a shore of fine sand, not white, not cream, not yellow, but a mixture of them all with the sheen of mica glittering in the sunshine as if the beach itself shone with a halo. Boys were shinning up the tall coconut palms that edged the beach, laughing and teasing and, every now and then, cutting a coconut and tossing it onto the shining sand. Behind the palms, the mountains rose to a sky of azure uncluttered with clouds.

Melanie loved their days at the beach and especially the two Saturdays when her father came too. He and her mother would each take one of her hands and walk out into the ocean further and further until they were almost swimming, with Melanie's feet splashing through the water like a mermaid's tail, until they were so far out from the shore that the water tickled her mother's chin and only the tips of her toes could touch the sand.

Then her mother would swim away, and back, and away and back, with barely a splash, while she and her father would frolic together in the sea, laughing and teasing and splashing and swimming and jumping. Melanie delighted in their games, particularly *Down at the Bottom of the Deep Blue Sea* or *ring-a-ring-a-roses*, but her most favourite thing of all was when she floated on her back while her father supported her from underneath. All she could feel was the flow of the water, soft as silk against her skin; all she could smell was the salty ozone that made her heart sing; all she could hear was the lapping of the waves in her ears and all she could see was an arc of perfect blue sky.

Safe and warm, happy and buoyant, all three of them at ease in the warm blue benevolent sea: what could be more wonderful? She wanted those days to go on forever.

Those halcyon days at the seashore were the happiest of Melanie's young life. But just a few months later, when she was walking to school wellington-boot-deep in snow, they seemed as fleeting as the thunder clouds in an African mid-day sky.

Even so, the memory of them would always warm her heart with endless joy.

What a Beautiful Sierra Leone

'How beautiful you look in that resplendent blue, white and green dress.
A ravishing African gown studded with gold and diamonds.
Sweet smelling hibiscus flowers and piquant tamarind trees,
dot the landscape of your loving demeanour.
As gentle winds tussle your palm-leaf tresses,
the deep blue Atlantic waters caress your graceful undulating beach-curves.
The humming birds and cooing doves are at peace in your paradise gardens,
while the fat earth-worms wallow in your rich black soil.'

Madani Barrie

Acknowledgements

Special thanks go to my daughters Sophie O'Sullivan and Laura Barber who were keen to have some record of my experiences as a young child travelling in a world that no longer exists. Their encouragement was a huge spur to try to capture the living essence of Africa, seen as only a child can.

To Susan Boss, Margaret Trowell, Tricia Oakland, Mary Upton, Colleen Guy, Patricia Marston, Keir Dellar, Fiona Beer, Joanne Burchfield-James, Jenny Coote, and Catherine Collingwood go my sincere thanks for your constant encouragement.

Christine Warrington and Vivien Ford deserve particular thanks for their skill and patience in helping with the proof-reading this of book. Any mistakes that remain are mine alone.

As always, my husband, Richard Eaton has helped me enormously in the editing and production of the final story. But not only that — he has encouraged me, fed me and brought me endless cups of coffee. Thank you, Richard.

While searching for information with which to round-out my childhood memories of Sierra Leone I found these websites helpful and informative: www.sierra-leone.org, www.freetowncity.com, and www.lionmountains.com

Particular thanks, too, go to Mandani Barrie who wrote the beautiful poem that ends the narrative of this book and to Peter Andersen for his endeavours on my behalf in searching for Mandani.

But most of all, thank you, my readers, for lending your eyes and ears to my story. I do hope you enjoyed reading it.

About the Author

As a small girl in 1956, Marion Eaton travelled to Sierra Leone with her parents, her father being the Resident Civil Engineer responsible for a project to reverse the flow of a river from its source in the Lion Mountains. To a child brought up in the English countryside, her stay in West Africa was a revelation. Everything about Sierra Leone was beautiful, despite the danger lurking hidden in the jungle, and the political unrest that would explode into civil war within a few decades. Notwithstanding the prejudices of the time, an abiding kinship developed between her and the African garden-boy who built her a house from native materials.

Marion now lives in the Sussex countryside with a very understanding husband, a very spoiled and lazy hound and a large rambling garden, all of which she attempts to keep in some semblance of order.

More information can be found at marioneaton.com.

A Note From the Author

Thank you very much for reading this novella. I do hope you enjoyed it.

If you would like to receive the occasional newsletter, please sign up for one on marioneaton.com. You may also like to follow me on Twitter @marioneaton and/or like my Facebook page. I would love to hear from you. Please mention this book and I will be pleased to send you a free short read in appreciation.

You may not know that honest reviews are of immense value to an author, so if you would give one at the Amazon website from which you bought the book, it would be of enormous help. And greatly appreciated. Thank you.

Other books published by Touchworks Ltd

The Elephants' Child
by **M.L. Eaton**

No 1 in the Faraway Lands Series

It is 1954 and Melanie is six years old. With her parents, she moves to Bombay, (now Mumbai) India, but, anxious and unsettled, she finds it difficult to make friends.
Entranced by the emotive beauty of her surroundings, she unexpectedly discovers the love and friendship that banish her loneliness.
At times sad and poignant but always enthralling and exhilarating, this is a story that captures the wonders of India as seen through the eyes and imagination of a young English girl.

'A gush of air bore the animal's spirit from her body. The earth quaked with the shock: after-tremors rocked the trees, rustling their leaves. Silence: bending trees slowly straightening. In the aftermath of death there was a great stillness. Even the calf was still now, frozen in shock as well as bound in ropes, silent in its cage. The silence stretched: and stretched further. Until slowly, slowly, men crept out from behind trees and undergrowth. Others descended from the treetops. The white man, who had fallen full length upon the ground, slowly rose and gathered up his gun.

Silent in her prison, the elephant calf grieved for her mother, her freedom, her kind. Never again, she intuited, would she be free to roam the green and sacred land. Never again would she watch a lazy bird-of-prey circle between the green jungle hills; never again would she play with her kind in the crystal waters of the creeks – squirting water, bathing, drinking, playing. Ever after, she would be at the mercy of man, this puny creature who would beat and poke the spirit from her, until she did his bidding always.'

When the Clocks Stopped
by M.L. Eaton
No 1 in the Mysterious Marsh Series

The long hot summer of 1976. The mysterious Romney Marsh in the South of England. Hazel Dawkins, a feisty young lawyer, takes maternity leave anticipating a period of tranquillity. Instead, the dreams begin. In them she encounters Annie, a passionate young woman whose romantic and tempestuous life was adventurously lived, more than two centuries previously, in the cottage that Hazel now occupies.

As their destinies entwine, Hazel not only confronts a terrifying challenge which parallels history, she finds herself desperately fighting for survival in a cruel and unforgiving age. Even more disturbing is the realisation that her battle will affect the future for those in the past whose fate is, as yet, unwritten.

Her only ally is Annie. Together they face events that echo through the centuries, events that are as violent and compelling as they are unexpected.

And, as the past collides with the present, the time for the birth of Hazel's child draws ever nearer.

Prologue

The silver light of a gibbous moon shimmers on the new green leaves of the ash tree. The horse stamps and jerks his head, jangling the bridle. I sway with the movement, soothing him instinctively. The sweetish smell of horse is thick about me as I wait at the crossroads. Stiff as I am in every joint and sinew, my body screams for me to dismount and stretch my legs, but I cannot. Some intuition, some sense of impending destiny, holds me motionless. I am aware it will not be long.

I flinch as the expectant hush is broken by the screech of an owl, eerie in the stillness that binds me to the saddle. She circles silently above me, seeking her prey. I watch until she glides away into the blackest shadows, where the sacred ash grove huddles beneath the escarpment.

My eyes seek the hallowed place where the Earth Mother is still honoured by man and maid on the sacred feast of Beltane; the ash grove to which they come at dawn, clad in white, and garlanded in green. May blossoms wreathe their brows as they stand side by side under a living canopy for their hand-clasping, their ceremony of rejoicing in union, the celebration of life itself in dance and song. This is the seven-treed sacred grove to which my beloved and I came not long ago; there we swore an oath to honour our love and there later, alone beneath the moon-silvered leaves we became one in the flesh.

It grows cold now, and I shiver. The horse pricks up his ears, listening intently. A small sound trembles towards me; perhaps no more than a fluctuation in the air current. Then the nightingale's exquisite song fills the air with beauty. It is the signal: Jack's signal.

I fire my weapon into the sky and wheel about, pulling sharply on the reins. We race off into the night. Lying close to the horse's back, my head beside his ear, I ride hard. For a moment or two, as we gather speed, I choose those places where the low light gleams through the covering of cloud. I catch the sound of hooves in swift pursuit and know I have been seen. Now I guide my good companion into the gloom of the darkest shadows, allowing him to choose his own footing on the causeway. He gallops on.

I risk a backward glimpse. Shapes pursue us; legless in the mist rising from the Marsh, centaurs ride hard in a bow-shaped line. The triumph and excitement of the men who chase me is almost palpable. How long were they lingering near the crossroads where I myself had waited?

I let the gelding have his head because he knows these levels well. His hooves drum into the earth and I crouch low in *the saddle, horse sweat hot-smelling in my nostrils. As I cling to his mane, I chance another glance but see nothing. I am sure we are gaining on our pursuers, but have they ridden yet into the trap where the Marsh is quicksand and will swallow horse and rider whole?*

The moon is hidden now and I have no bearings. All I hear is a thrumming, thrumming, thrumming — and I know not whether it is my heart beating in my ears or the sound of pursuit. All I can do is ride.

When the Tide Turned
by **M.L. Eaton**

No 2 in the Mysterious Marsh Series

It is August 1976 and an oppressive heat hangs over Romney Marsh in the South East corner of England. Soon after the birth of her daughter, Hazel Dawkins, a young lawyer, is unexpectedly asked to return to work. No sooner has she agreed than she discovers that a dark force threatens both her family and her country; and before long, the past and present intertwine in a rising tide of horrifying events. Haunted by terrifying images, she knows that she must uncover secrets from the past if she is to avert a catastrophe that will destroy all that she holds dear.

What draws her to the painting depicting a sudden storm at sea on a night in 1803 as Napoleon prepares to invade England? What is the secret of the man pegged down to die on the incoming tide? As Hazel seeks the answers to these questions, she faces evil and intrigue, her life and that of her baby daughter, threatened at every turn.

<<<<>>>>

Printed in Great Britain
by Amazon.co.uk, Ltd.,
Marston Gate.